THE MYSTERY OF
LUCIEN DELORME

"It seemed to Hester that she had seen this man somewhere
before."

THE INTERNATIONAL ADVENTURE LIBRARY

THREE OWLS EDITION

The MYSTERY of LUCIEN DELORME

BY

GUY DE TÉRAMOND

TRANSLATED BY

MARY J. SAFFORD

W. R. CALDWELL & CO.
NEW YORK

CONTENTS

v

Contents

PART III

THE MAN WHO SEES THROUGH WALLS

PART I

THE RAJAH'S JEWELS

CHAPTER I

THE ARMELIN BOARDING-HOUSE

ON the nineteenth of May, 191—, about five o'clock in the afternoon, a cab left the Quai d'Orsay with a passenger whose little trunk had been put on the driver's seat.

The latter had undoubtedly discovered that his fare had arrived in Paris from the provinces, for every now and then he obligingly pointed out, with the end of his whip, the various buildings past which the horse was slowly trotting:

"The Palace of the Legion of Honor . . . the Chamber of Deputies . . . the Invalides . . . the Zouave on the Pont de l'Alma that disappeared entirely under the water during the last inundations . . ."

The traveler, however, appeared to pay little attention to the enumeration, remaining absorbed in deep reflections.

He wore a chestnut-colored suit, in good style, but not especially well cut, and a soft gray felt hat. Apparently he was still young, with a little fair mustache shading his upper lip, of middle height, as well as could be judged, and by no means corpulent. He would even have been quite a good-looking fellow but for the black spectacles astride of his nose, which gave his face the mysterious expression possessed by all persons whose eyes cannot be seen.

Yet, whenever the driver addressed him, he thanked him politely, glanced absently at the building, and instantly relapsed into his reverie; evidently he was not greatly interested in Paris, though he was seeing it for the first time.

At the end of half an hour, the cab stopped suddenly at the corner of the Avenue Mozart and the Rue de la Cure, opposite a small private house just at the angle, projecting like a prow from an immense block of dwellings. Three stories high, built of brick and roofed with slates, it was quite fashionable in appearance, somewhat in the Louis XIII style, modernized, with no great taste, by its architect.

At the right of the door, on a square of black marble, were these words in gilt letters:

FAMILY HOUSE

The trade of family boarding-houses which, on account of the vicinity of the Bois de Boulogne, still flourishes in Passy and Auteuil, had taken possession, in its turn, of this little dwelling, which otherwise would have been difficult to rent.

"Here we are, sir," said the cabman.

The traveler left the vehicle, asked the driver to wait a moment, and entered the Family House.

A little servant, with one of the coquettish lace caps worn by English maids, hurried forward to meet him.

"Can I speak to the landlady?"

"Certainly, sir."

She opened the door of the office to let him pass.

"Will you walk in? I'll tell Madame . . ."

She ran upstairs.

The young man had not had time to examine the room, which resembled all others used for the same purpose,—a set of bells, engravings hung on the walls, green velvet furniture, and in the center a table loaded with pamphlets, where a bouquet of peonies, in a tall pink vase, was just fading,—when Madame Armelin entered.

She was a lady of uncertain age, dressed in black, whose gray hair gave her an appearance of great dignity. She came forward, smiling pleasantly.

"What can I do for you, sir?"

"Madame," replied the young man, "your fam-

5

ily boarding-house has been recommended to me by one of my friends, M. Philibert Thierry of Chartres."

This was the first time Madame Armelin had ever heard the name, but she took care to show no sign that she did not remember it perfectly.

"He told me that the cooking was excellent, the rooms neat, and the quiet of the house absolute."

A man who speaks of one's house in terms so flattering must be a gentleman: Madame Armelin's sympathy was instantly won for the stranger.

"All this is perfectly correct, sir," she answered modestly.

"I value especially the last point, Madame. The most absolute quiet. I have come to Paris to consult an eminent specialist for . . ."

He hesitated an instant, and then continued:

"For nervous troubles from which I have suffered for some time, and to take the treatment he prescribes. So you see that entire quiet is the first necessity!"

"You will find it here, sir. The house is famous for that, M. Albert Thierry——"

"Philibert."

"Philibert Thierry must have told you that I took no noisy people in my house."

The stranger nodded. He liked this Family

House. The landlady appeared like an honest person. His friend had not deceived him; he would undoubtedly be very comfortable during his stay.

"Now I should like to know your terms, Madame."

"How long do you expect to stay?"

"I don't know. Probably more than a month. When one begins treatments one never knows when they will come to an end."

"If you are to remain at least a month, I will charge you ten francs a day."

"Wine included?"

"And service also—nothing more to be paid! Three meals, breakfast served in your room, if you wish. As to the room, I'll give you one of my very best, on the second story, with two windows overlooking the Avenue Mozart. On one side there is an old American lady, who rarely makes any noise, on the other, the next house; the chambers overhead just now are unoccupied."

"All this will be just the thing!" replied the young man. "I'll go and pay my cabman. Please have my trunk brought up."

His hand was already on the door handle when he turned back:

"By the way, Madame, are the meals served at little separate tables?"

7

"No, sir. There is only one large table, around which all the boarders meet. But there are only three now."

"But I really must eat alone. My head is very tired, and the noise of conversation makes me suffer intensely."

Unexpected patrons are not allowed to go for such a trifle.

"You shall be served at a small table," Madame Armelin replied, "only I shall have to charge you a franc extra," she added timidly, ready to yield the point if he refused.

"Very well."

While the landlady was calling the porter to take the trunk, the young man went to pay the cab-driver.

"A ten sous tip for showing you all the buildings in Paris," muttered the man between his teeth; "it's plain that you're from the country."

Five minutes later the new boarder was settled in his room, already putting his clothes in the wardrobe.

This little task completed, he sat down in an armchair near the mantelpiece, drew off his boots, which he exchanged for slippers and laying his dark glasses near him he closed his eyes, sighing comfortably: "Ah!"

Someone knocked suddenly at the door.

He hastily put on the glasses and, going to open it, found the little maid, with a register in her hand.

"Will you please write your name, sir?" she asked.

He took the pen she held out to him, and in a firm hand wrote:

Name: Lucien Delorme. *Profession:* student. *Coming from:* Eu-la-Mouillette (Lower Seine).

Madame Armelin's family boarding-house, at this time, was especially quiet; the three persons to whom she had alluded were somewhat advanced in years and sedate in disposition.

First there was the American lady, Mrs. Tankery, whose room adjoined the young man's, a widow about sixty, lively and agreeable, whose only fault was making herself a little ridiculous with the rouge she put on her face, her somewhat pronounced blonde wig, and unduly juvenile costumes.

She had come to board with Madame Armelin while waiting for her son to settle up some business in lard and hogs in Chicago, before arriving to live permanently with her in Paris.

Mrs. Tankery drove all day in the Bois de Boulogne in a carriage driven by a trusty old coachman; if it rained, she went to the Museums, the exhibitions, and the great shops, returning

9

just in time to dress for dinner. For it was an ineradicable mania with her to appear in full dress every evening; she would not have gone down to the dining-room except in a low-necked gown, with all her jewels.

These jewels represented in themselves a little fortune; a diamond necklace, pearl earrings, bracelets, rings, nothing was lacking. When an American woman is rich she means to show it.

Madame Armelin had offered vainly to keep them in her safe, not intending, according to the rule printed in large type in the office, "*to be responsible for articles of value unless placed in her care.*" Mrs. Tankery had refused to part with her jewels.

"Isn't your house safe?" she answered obstinately.

"Certainly, but . . ."

"Well, why do you want me to deprive myself of my only pleasure? Besides, there's no danger of being robbed. I put them under my pillow."

The second guest was the Guatemalan general, Domingo y Lopez, a little old man with an olive complexion, and jet black mustache, who always rolled his eyes fiercely and wore in his buttonhole a multicolored rosette, in which all the hues of the rainbow seemed to have mingled.

Why had he left his country? What had he

10

come to do in Paris? For the three months he
had lived with her, Madame Armelin had never
been able to solve this mystery.

To hear him talk, his object was to study something. But what? The new French cannon? The
operation of the automobile street-sweepers?
Or the statistics of births?

The most certain thing was that he received a
voluminous mail from his distant country and
that all the letters which came to him in Paris
bore the stamp of the Guatemalan legation.

At meals, he filled the difficult position of host
and obligingly related his exploits, which, as may
be supposed, were both numerous and varied.

In the suppression of the last insurrection,
especially, he had covered himself with glory.

"I took four thousand prisoners, men, women,
children, and others. To make an example, I
decided to shoot them all—only as there was a
lack of ammunition I fastened them one behind the
other, so that the same ball would do for several
at once!"

"O General!" cried sensitive Mrs. Tankery,
shuddering with horror.

"Those are the laws of war, Madame!" he an-
swered with a look intended to strike terror.
"An eye for an eye, a tooth for a tooth. When
I dashed forward on the battlefield, at the head

of the Government troops, they did not trouble themselves to aim, no, no, no pity! Ten thousand at once!"

"But, General," Madame Armelin said gently, "just now you said four thousand."

"I forgot . . . there were so many, and every day, it began again. That was the time that our enthusiastic fellow-citizens wanted to make me president of the Republic. I refused. I preferred to come to Paris."

While . speaking, he twirled his black mustache between his yellow fingers, doubtless thinking that this was really the safest statement.

The third boarder was an old professor, a childhood friend of Madame Armelin, in whose house he had settled after his retirement and who regarded him more as an aged relative than a patron.

He spent his days at work in his room, appearing in the dining-room only at meal hours, as if nothing in the world possessed any interest to him outside of his books.

His courtesy was extreme. He listened obligingly to the general's braggadocio, and having grown sceptical with age concerning Guatemalan revolutions, he was very careful neither to question nor to contradict him, thereby winning a firm place in his favor.

He emerged from his usual silence only to explain to Mrs. Tankery, with tireless patience, the obscure beauties of the French language and to endeavor to rid her transatlantic jargon of the solecisms, barbarisms, and pleonasms, which blossomed in it as numberlessly as violets in a wood.

In this occupation he was completely at home. Recovering his past youth he devoted himself to it every instant with an assiduity which somewhat set the general's nerves on edge over these perpetual lessons:

"For my part, I want to know no language except that of the battlefield! Boom! Boom! Seven thousand at one round!"

"O General," shuddered Madame Armelin admiringly, "you are terrible!"

Dinner was invariably over at nine o'clock, and a game of whist immediately followed, Madame Armelin being the fourth. It was the dull season, and she gave herself a vacation during the evenings.

At ten o'clock the game ended, and everybody went to bed. Half an hour later the Family House was buried in the deepest slumber.

The young stranger did not wish to bring any disturbance into these patriarchal customs. When dinner was over, he went back to his room.

13

Madame Armelin, through courtesy, had offered him her seat at the whist table, but he had declined, saying that he did not know any game of cards.

"He is right," said the general. "At his age I didn't care about this nonsense either. I had won three battles."

"Were you already a general?" asked the American.

"Yes, Madame. At sixteen I volunteered . . . at seventeen I was a captain, at eighteen a colonel, the next day a general."

"How rapidly you advance in your country!"

"That proves we have only brave men there!" He rolled his eyes fiercely.

"At any rate," said Madame Armelin, who prided herself upon judging people by their appearance, "this poor boy looks very ill. Have you noticed the sad expression of his face? No doubt he is discouraged about his health? So young, too, isn't it pitiful?"

Curiosity had led her to try skillfully, several times, to find out something—whether he had consulted a specialist, if he had commenced his·treatment, if he was feeling better?

But young Delorme civilly eluded all these questions, seeming obstinately determined not to enter into any details on this subject. Once only, having come in very late to dinner, he had apologized by saying that his physician had detained him longer in consultation than he had expected.

But the most extraordinary thing about him was his black glasses. These seemed to be part of himself. Never did he lay them aside, from morning till night, nor probably from night till morning, since the waiter who entered his room at any hour, had always seen them on his nose.

They gave him a peculiar appearance, half Quaker, half chauffeur.

"It's a queer idea, all the same," the Guatemalan general had exclaimed, "for a young man to muffle himself up like that."

"My dear Señor Domingo y Lopez," Madame Armelin had replied, with her most obsequious smile, "it is your glory that dazzles him!"

This peculiarity, moreover, had not escaped the eyes of the servants in Family House, and it sometimes became the subject of their conversation.

"I'd like to know anyway," said one of the maids, "whether his eyes are black or blue."

"At any rate," answered the other, who waited on the newcomer at his little table, "they must be very bad, poor fellow. Day before yesterday, in taking the bread from the basket I was holding, his cuff caught the glasses and dragged them from his nose. If you had seen him! He jumped and threw up his hands as though he had just had a blow full in the face!"

"He's a queer stick!" the waiter agreed. "You know a telegram came for him the other evening. I knocked at his door, and, as he did not answer, I pushed it open. For a wonder, it wasn't locked. I'll give you a hundred guesses to tell what he was doing . . . He had drawn the curtains of his bed and inside he was using two little electric pocket lamps. Of course, when I came in he put them out. Now, what do you think of that?"

CHAPTER II

THE NIGHT OF JUNE FIRST, 191—

L UCIEN DELORME had been the guest of the family boarding-house in the Avenue Mozart for nearly a fortnight when a dramatic event suddenly disturbed his peace of mind.

Every morning, at nine o'clock, Lucie, the maid on the second story, took the American lady a pitcher of hot water and a waiter on which was arranged her breakfast, always consisting of tea, preserves, and toast browned to a turn.

But this morning she knocked at the door in vain; there was no answer.

"Mrs. Tankery is still asleep!" she murmured, and went down to the office, listening for the bell that would soon summon her back.

Ten o'clock struck, then eleven.

"It's certainly very queer that Mrs. Tankery hasn't waked yet," thought the maid.

She went up and knocked again more loudly.

The same silence reigned. Then, seized with a sense of vague anxiety, she hurried to tell Madame Armelin.

17

The latter was also astonished. Mrs. Tankery rose early. Never before had she slept so late.

"We must persist," she said. And she followed Lucie.

But her repeated calls also remained useless, and she was just deciding to risk a peep through the keyhole when the Guatemalan general appeared. He was going to take a walk around the lakes as he did every morning for an appetizer.

He was informed, in a few words, of the situation; the familiarity with battlefields had given him a spirit of prompt decision.

"There's no need of hesitation," he said. "We must go in, at any rate. Perhaps Mrs. Tankery is ill. Send for a locksmith."

Lucie was preparing to obey when, while speaking, the general unconsciously turned the handle of the door, which swung wide open. It was not even locked.

Then at the unexpected spectacle before them, the three could not help uttering an exclamation of horror.

In the center of the apartment lay the American lady, her face against the floor, her arms extended, in the midst of a pool of blood which, gushing from a terrible wound in the neck, had

18

gradually transformed her chemise into a red winding sheet.

"O Heaven!" cried the general. And the pitiless thunderbolt of war who shot down his enemies by thousands, with all the refinements of cruelty, turned sick.

Meanwhile, Madame Armelin did not lose her wits; and as Lucie was already moving toward the body, she ordered:

"Don't touch anything and inform the police at once. Jump into a taxicab, the station is on the Place de Passy. But," she sighed, under her breath, when the maid had started on a run, "I did not want such a thing to happen in my house."

Then she busied herself with the general.

Fifteen minutes later the commissary of police of the quarter and his secretary alighted from an automobile and, after having had the doors of the house closed, and forbidden anyone to enter or leave it, they proceeded to make the first investigations, while awaiting the arrival of the head of the detective service, who had been notified by telephone.

At the first glance no one could doubt that robbery was the motive of the crime.

The wardrobe, the desk, the bureau had been broken open; the articles and underclothing which they contained were scattered in disorder about the room; the first object of the murderers had been to lay hands on the unfortunate American's jewels.

They were certainly people of good taste. If they had neglected articles of no value, they had taken care to cut the old lace from Mrs. Tankery's evening gowns and had not left behind several valuable trinkets which she had purchased since her arrival in Paris.

"Poor woman!" murmured Madame Armelin, "I had warned her that it was imprudent to keep so many valuable things in her possession; we never ought to tempt people, no matter how trusting we may be!"

At this moment M. Clamart, the head of the Detective Bureau, arrived, accompanied by a legal physician and followed by employees of M. Bertillon, with their apparatus for taking the finger prints left by the villains.

"The crime is signed," he said, after an instant's examination; "it was committed by professionals who are not experimenting. Everything has been planned in advance and admirably executed."

He added: "The American lady was sound asleep when, during the night, the assassins came from outside by a way that is yet to be discovered, cut out one of the window panes with a diamond, passed an arm through the opening and slid back the window fastening, then they had nothing more to do except to enter the room.

"Without the least pause they rushed to the bed, whose exact position they knew, and by a well-aimed blow of a poniard, one of them severed the unfortunate woman's carotid artery before she had time to utter a single cry, bespattering the sheets with a trail of blood."

Had she then mechanically taken a few steps to fall in the middle of the room? Or had the murderers laid their victim's corpse there in order—not knowing where she was in the habit of hiding her jewels—to be able to search the mattresses more conveniently?

At any rate, it was not surprising that, the story below being unoccupied at night, the dull sound of the fall of a body on a carpet should have wakened no one.

These first investigations having been rapidly made, while the commissary was busy in searching outside for the way by which the criminals had succeeded in reaching Mrs. Tankery's window, the chief of the Detective Bureau, leaving the physician and the employees of the anthropometrical bureau to work in the room, was engaged in questioning Madame Armelin's servants.

The latter could give no useful information. They occupied rooms on the ground floor, almost in the basement, adjoining the kitchen, the office, and the linen room. They had gone to bed as usual, about eleven o'clock, when their work was over, and had heard nothing suspicious.

These servants, moreover, were trustworthy people who had been a long time in the service of the head of the Family House. So any complicity on their part could at once be eliminated.

Besides, the magistrate's very positive belief was that the crime had not been committed by individuals associated in any way with the family boarding-house, but rather by the ruffians who are always on the watch for a profitable job and lie in wait for foreigners whom they suppose to be rich, in the hope of finding some day an opportunity to rob them.

But who?

Since Mrs. Tankery's arrival in Paris she had received no visitors, all her afternoons were spent driving in the Bois de Boulogne or in going through the great shops. The cabman who drove her was an excellent man who had been for twenty-five years in the service of the same employer; it was improbable to believe that he had played, in this crime, the part of instigator.

"Now let us take up your boarders," said the

magistrate, addressing Madame Armelin, for whom he had sent to meet him in the hotel office. "How many have you?"

"There are three left, as my register shows," she answered. "First, Señor Domingo y Lopez . . ."

Then, at the official's questioning look, she continued:

"A Guatemalan general who has been in Paris six months—a braggart—a great talker—but an excellent man at heart, incapable, I am sure, of committing the smallest crime. He was with us when we discovered Mrs. Tankery's body. It made him fairly ill . . ."

"And the others?"

"A friend whom I have known since my childhood, an old man whose great age shelters him from all suspicion. He has been my guest for more than three years, and I will answer for him as I would for myself."

"Very well. And the third?"

"He is a young man, M. Delorme, who came to my house about a fortnight ago——"

"Ah!" cried the official, suddenly interested. "Where is this young man from?"

"From the provinces, from Eu, I believe."

"For what purpose is he here?"

"To be treated by a great specialist for nervous troubles from which he suffers, he told me."

"What impression has he made upon you?"

"Why—really, a good one. He is well-bred, polite to everybody, regular in his habits, only a little shy, and does not associate with anybody in the household."

"You have not noticed anything unusual about him?"

"Nothing; except that he never took off his black glasses."

"Didn't that surprise you?"

"No. I thought he had weak eyes. My poor father wore them, for that reason, during the last ten years of his life."

"And where did he sleep?"

"In the next room to poor Mrs. Tankery."

"Ah! Did he ask you for it?"

"He asked me to give him one where he would not be disturbed by noise from his neighbors. That one met his requirements best."

The official remained silent a moment, pondering.

"Come," he said, after an instant, "summon up your recollections, Madame. During the fortnight that this young man has been your guest, has nothing, absolutely nothing, attracted your attention?"

24

"Really nothing. Wait, though, Monsieur. One single thing, perhaps, but it was so unimportant."

"Never mind, tell me."

"He came here, giving as a reference a person whose name was unknown to me. A M. Thery or Tierry, of Chartres. I pretended to know him, of course. After all, it was possible that the gentleman might have stayed here. I cannot remember exactly the names of all my boarders since I have been established twenty years. Though, still," she added in a low tone, as if making an apology to herself, "my memory is yet good."

"You see! He wanted to win your confidence, and make sure that you would not refuse to receive him!"

"How could I have supposed all that!" sighed the worthy woman.

"And now, on what terms did he stand with Mrs. Tankery?"

"I don't think he has ever spoken to her. One day I offered to present him. He refused, saying he had no desire to make the acquaintance of that "old caricature." He even added that such a display of jewelry was ridiculous and would only lead to her being murdered."

"It wasn't difficult for him to show himself so good a prophet! Well, Madame, will you ask this M. Delorme to come and talk with me a moment?"

"That is impossible."

"Why?"

"He has gone out."

The questioner started up.

"Gone out! And at what time?"

"I don't know. He had already left his room when the waiter went in to carry his breakfast."

"So no one has seen him to-day, and consequently he may very easily have gone in the middle of the night?"

"Certainly."

"And I suppose he was not in the habit of taking such early departures?"

"This is really the first time."

At that moment the commissary of police returned, and Madame Armelin withdrew, completely upset.

"Well," said the head of the detective service, "have you found anything?"

"We discovered along the wall some fresh scratches which seemed to confirm the conjecture that the assassins came through the window by means of a rope . . ."

"Thrown from inside by an accomplice, an accomplice who could be no one except one of the boarders in Family House, even the victim's next door neighbor. The investigation has already taken an important step, hasn't it, my dear Commissary?"

"You are entitled to all the credit, sir."

"Hum!—You see, whatever precautions the most skillful criminals take, it is rare that they do not leave behind something that betrays them."

And he began to inform his fellow official rapidly of all the deductions that Madame Armelin's examination had suggested.

According to him, there could be no doubt, and the genesis of the crime was thus established: some individual came, with a false reference, into a family boarding-house where someone had told him lived an elderly foreigner who had valuable jewels. He had taken care to disguise his face with black glasses and to pretend he did not wish to speak to anyone, so that he could not drop any imprudent word. For a fortnight he studied at his leisure the habits of his victim, then, sure of his business, one night he introduced his accomplice, and the deed was done.

"Perfectly logical," replied the commissary, "only . . ."

"Only what?"

"The only thing I don't understand is the broken pane. Since he had merely to admit his accomplice through his own window, what was the use of that?"

"Those details will be elucidated later by the examining magistrate; perhaps simply to avoid having the first suspicions rest upon him, and thus give himself time to escape. Meanwhile, do you search the fellow's room, while I will try to obtain, from the head of the establishment and the servants, an accurate personal description. Then we will set our spies upon his track without delay. In such a case minutes are precious. Ask Madame Armelin to return here."

But it was not she who, a few minutes after, entered the room; to his great astonishment, the chief of the detectives saw Lucien Delorme himself appear.

"You wish to see me, sir?" he asked.

With a bound the officer was between the young man and the door, to prevent any attempt at flight, and abruptly exclaimed:

"Up with your hands."

Delorme, taken by surprise, mechanically obeyed; then, instantly recovering his coolness, he said:

"What does this mean?"

"I am the chief of the detective service . . ."

"That is possible, sir, but is it a reason for speaking to me with such rudeness? Set your

mind at rest, I am not armed, and if you wish
me to answer you, I must beg you to adopt a
different manner."

The police officer was accustomed to protestations of this sort; all criminals began by assuming a lofty tone. So, without allowing himself
to be intimidated, or removing his eyes from the
young man, that he might be ready to spring
upon him at the first movement, he retorted:

"Come, no useless tales. You know what I
am talking about?"

"No."

"The murder that was committed here last
night."

"What murder?"

"Mrs. Tankery's."

"Mrs. Tankery has been murdered? Last
night? O poor woman!"

"You knew nothing about it?" persisted M.
Clamart, looking at him with a searching glance.

"No. I went out early this morning, doubtless before the discovery of the crime."

"Contrary to your habits, and without taking
time to eat your breakfast?"

"Yes, Dr. Guéroult, who is attending me, asked
me to come to his office this morning before eating."

While he was speaking, the detective nodded

29

silently, thinking: "Here is a clever fellow! Now I understand the reason for the broken pane. This was the first part of his alibi. His visit to the doctor is the second. This is all skillfully planned, and I shall not take him unawares."

"So it is a mere coincidence!" The officer went on ironically. "But suppose we should talk a little, now, about Mrs. Tankery? It seems that you predicted she would be murdered?"

"Not at all, I simply said, as well as I remember, that it was imprudent, on her part, to make such a display of all her jewels."

"Did you know their value?"

"I had heard Madame Armelin say that they represented a little fortune. I am, however, a very incompetent judge."

"And you were not ignorant that she always kept them in her room?"

"I . . ."

Suddenly he stopped.

"Pardon me. Questions like these!—Surely you could not suspect me of being connected in any way with this horrible crime?"

The detective looked him in the eyes and said slowly:

"Lucien Delorme, you are one of Mrs. Tankery's murderers!"

The young man's face expressed utter amazement. He turned frightfully pale and seemed to totter, while his lips stammered confused words. But he gradually regained his self-control and, recovering his coolness, energetically protested:

"I, a murderer? The charge is ridiculous. Why, I did not leave my room last night. And, besides, for what reason should I have killed this poor lady?"

"Come, Delorme," answered the detective, in a conciliatory tone. "I did not say that it was you who dealt the blows—but one can sometimes be led by certain circumstances—one doesn't refuse to keep watch—or to throw a rope out of the window, believing that the plan is merely robbery."

"But I have done nothing of the sort—I swear it. I knew nothing of the crime. I was coming home quietly to breakfast when, at the foot of the staircase, I met Madame Armelin, who sent me here . . ."

He interrupted himself suddenly, passed his hand across his forehead with a nervous gesture, and murmured:

"And yet, yes . . . I do know something. I must free my conscience by telling you . . . I could not believe it . . . but since Mrs. Tankery has been murdered, it must be true."

The detective concealed a smile of triumph.

31

He had his man, for he had placed him under the necessity of defending himself. Now he need only lead him skillfully on to draw him to confession. The matter was settled.

He courteously motioned the young man to a seat.

"Sit down, my dear M. Delorme, and tell me about it."

The young man began his story:

"Neither closely nor remotely have I been connected with this terrible crime. If you have the slightest suspicion of that sort, the inquest will establish the truth. And yet—I know how the crime was committed . . . I saw it committed as plainly as if I had been in Mrs. Tankery's room."

At the recollection, large drops of perspiration stood on his forehead, and his hands trembled violently.

"Will you have a glass of rum?" asked the detective obligingly.

But, without hearing him, the young man continued:

"There were two murderers—one tall, the other short—each carried two revolvers—the taller had a ring on the ring-finger of the right hand—the shorter man had a watch in his left vest pocket, and a dagger between his teeth. They

32

came in through the window, having crept to the apartment along the walls. The tall man had a dark lantern, which he turned upon the bed. Just at that moment his companion sprang forward and, with a metal cord, strangled his victim, who turned over and fell in the middle of the room. Then they rummaged everywhere . . . pieces of money rolled on the floor but they did not pick them up. The tall man, however, put in his pocket, the inner pocket of his overcoat or jacket, a silver statuette that stood on the night table. Now, if you wish, I can give you a special detail which perhaps will enable you to recognize the murderers. The tall man formerly received a bullet in the head which could not be extracted, and the short one, too, but his is in the leg. Finally, they went out as they came in, through the window. My clock struck three, and I fell asleep again."

"Fell asleep again!" cried the detective, who up to this moment had listened unmoved to the strange story. "But why didn't you call for help?"

"I thought myself the victim of a nightmare. It required your story of Mrs. Tankery's murder to make me perceive I had not been dreaming."

The chief of the Detective Bureau remained silent an instant. This man was evidently making fun of him. Should he take offense or show him the absurdity of such a system of defense by making him contradict himself? He decided on the latter course.

"Your story is certainly very ingenious, sir," he replied. "Unfortunately it errs in one essential point. Mrs. Tankery was not strangled. Her carotid artery was severed. The blood that flooded the room, streaming from a wound in the neck, abundantly proves it."

The young man reflected, as if he were trying to materialize his recollections; his hands made a gesture in the air.

"No . . . no . . ." he repeated, "she was strangled . . . and with a cord which could have been nothing but metal."

"Come, sir, let us have no more of this nonsense!" exclaimed the detective, feeling his patience about to desert him.

Just then the door of the office opened, and the physician entered.

"You have come precisely at the right time, Doctor," exclaimed the magistrate. "This gentleman and I do not entirely agree on the subject of the crime of which he asserts he was a witness —a telepathic witness," he added sarcastically. "Will you be kind enough to tell us the result of your discoveries?"

"Gladly. In the first place the victim's death appears to have occurred about three o'clock in the morning."

"Well!" said Delorme triumphantly, without noticing the step the detective took toward him.

"Moreover, she was strangled."

"Strangled?"

"With a steel wire, and with such force that the carotid artery was severed completely, as if by a razor . . ."

He had not finished the sentence when the detective's hand was laid upon Lucien Delorme's shoulder.

"I arrest you, in the name of the Law!"

CHAPTER III

A SENSATIONAL REWARD

NINE o'clock was striking. Night was closing in. One by one, the gas lamps were lighted in the gathering dusk, which they pierced with their little blinking eyes. The Avenue Mozart was deserted. Pedestrians preferred the neighboring Bois to the dusty asphalt, scorched all day by the rays of a burning sun.

After having been, since morning, the object of the curiosity of the whole quarter where the news had flashed like a trail of powder, and the gathering place of all the journalists in the capital who were in quest of sensational reporting, the little house had finally recovered a quiet appearance.

Mrs. Tankery's body had been removed, and her room sealed. The boarders had gone up to their rooms immediately after dinner, feeling no heart for their daily game—especially with one of their number dead—while all through Paris the newsboys were crying the exciting headlines of their papers:

THE CRIME IN THE AVENUE MOZART
MURDER OF A RICH AMERICAN WOMAN
AN ARREST!

The servants, sitting before the door, talking in low tones, were enjoying the open air.

"You see," said Lucie, "that man with his way of hiding his face didn't seem to me of great account, and I wasn't much surprised when I heard that he was one of the murderers!"

"Nor I," the waiter agreed, "a fellow who kept shut up in his room all day! Is that natural? Perhaps he was planning his deed. If I had been the mistress I should have been suspicious!"

"At any rate," said the second maid, "he's caught. And I hope they'll make the rascal pay for it! How do you suppose foreigners will come to Paris if they are not safe here? Such stories won't help business and, without the foreigners . . ."

She suddenly stopped the lecture on social economy she was commencing. A cab had just stopped in front of Family House, and the mouths of the three servants opened in astonishment at the sight of the person who got out of it.

The man was Lucien Delorme.

"What!" cried the waiter, unable to believe his eyes, "have they let him go?"

"Oh," replied Lucie, "those people have more than one trick in their heads."

And, leaving her companions to their bewilderment, she ran to the office to tell Madame Armelin.

"Madame! Madame!" she called out of breath, "here he comes!"

Madame Armelin was just making out poor Mrs. Tankery's bill for the use of her heirs, for she was a woman of system.

"Who?" she asked, raising her head.

"The murderer . . ."

"What murderer?"

"The man with the black glasses."

Madame Armelin sprang to her feet.

"Good Lord! He has escaped!"

"I don't know, Madame. He's just getting out of a cab. Shall I call the police?"

But Madame Armelin had recovered a little composure and, conquering her excitement, she said:

"Keep quiet, Lucie, don't be so upset. I will go and speak to him."

"Oh, Madame, take care, what if he should try some other wicked deed."

Her mistress made a soothing gesture, and

was just going to meet the young man when the latter entered the office.

"You, sir?" she cried, disconcerted, in spite of herself, by his sudden appearance.

"Why, yes, Madame."

"You have been set at liberty?"

"An hour ago. I will not say with apologies, for it seems that even when in error, justice owes none, but the examining magistrate could not help yielding to the evidence and, in spite of the chief of the Detective Bureau, perceived that I could have had nothing to do with your boarder's murder."

Then, anticipating his hostess's questions, he rapidly gave her a few explanations.

At his urgent entreaty, the authorities had telephoned to Eu to obtain information about him and questioned Dr. Guéroult, who had stated that he had really requested his patient to come early that morning, and to come fasting.

"It is no fault of mine," he continued, "if no one in your house saw me leave my room at precisely half-past seven. Fortunately, the honest cabman whom I hailed at the corner of the Rue de la Cure, and whose number, luckily, I had kept, came to testify that he saw me come out of the house and took me in his cab at that hour!"

39

"Come, now," the examining magistrate had said to him, by way of consolation, "what queer idea induced you to tell all that ridiculous story to M. Clamart?"

"I admit that I was wrong," Delorme had answered. "But what can you expect? The news of Mrs. Tankery's murder had so upset me that I mistook for reality the strange nightmare in which I believed I was witnessing all the details and which, through some incomprehensible anticipation, coincided with the truth!"

"Well, my friend," the magistrate said kindly. "Off with you, and, above all, don't begin again to make fun of the police; another time you might fare worse."

Madame Armelin listened with a beating heart to this interesting story. She would have liked to question him further, but Delorme did not seem inclined to say more. He had talked too much to the chief of the detective service, and henceforth, he intended to keep cautiously on his guard.

He merely informed his hostess that he meant to leave her the next morning.

"What!" she exclaimed, "you are going? Are not you comfortable here?"

"Certainly, Madame. But after what has occurred, you will understand that it would be impossible for me to remain in a house where I feel I am regarded with suspicion."

"Why should you think that?"

"Well, Madame, if M. Clamart had not received information concerning me which was as damaging as it was incorrect, do you suppose he would ever have had the idea that I could have been connected with the horrible crime?"

"But who could have given it?" cried Madame Armelin, with sincere indignation.

"I don't know. And I have not even any desire to know. But I am going, that is all. Besides," he added, "if I wanted to remain longer it would be impossible."

Deep sadness, a tone of discouragement suddenly tinged his voice, as he went on:

"The doctors can do nothing for me . . . it would be necessary to undergo a serious operation, the result of which is doubtful . . . and I have not the courage to submit to it . . . I am going back to my mother in Eu . . . and what must happen will happen."

"Under these circumstances, sir, I should be unwilling to urge you. But," she instantly continued, "if you have any friend who is coming to Paris, I should be greatly obliged if you would recommend my house."

"You may be sure of that. I shall be glad

41

to say that your cooking is excellent, your rooms unusually neat, and that guests enjoy absolute quiet under your roof. I will even add that you sometimes offer them entirely unexpected mental diversions!"

Madame Armelin did not hear, or pretended not to understand.

"One thing more, Madame," said the young man, turning toward her, as he was leaving the room. "I shall take the eleven o'clock train. Until then I wish no one to be admitted. I will receive neither journalists nor reporters."

"They have come already."

"I suppose so, and that is why I am making the request. I need complete rest after the excitement through which I have passed to-day! Ah, you may believe that people don't easily forget a day's imprisonment on suspicion, in the police station!"

But while, worn out by fatigue, Lucien Delorme quickly fell asleep, the news of his return spread through the whole house, causing a profound sensation.

The first thought of each was that they had done right to release the young man if he were not guilty. But was this certain? After all, was that ever certain? If he were really entirely above suspicion, why had the head of the Detective Bureau had him arrested? Then did not this haste to leave the boarding-house testify against him, by showing that he considered it prudent to go away as quickly as possible from the scene of the crime?

By common consent it was agreed that the whole affair was not yet clear and, if he was profiting by the momentary doubt, it would be wise to wait before uttering any decision.

So, in spite of everything, Madame Armelin did not feel perfectly reassured about sleeping under the same roof with her young lodger. The old professor recommended his soul to God when he went to bed. As to the general, after loudly declaring that he had seen much more singular things and that he was afraid of nothing, he barricaded himself in his room by pushing all the furniture against the door.

Lucien Delorme was still sleeping a heavy, restful slumber when, toward nine o'clock, the waiter's repeated knocking roused him with a start.

"What is it?" he asked angrily.

"Someone in the drawing-room wants to see you."

"Let him go to the devil! I will see no one, you know that very well."

"He says it is absolutely necessary for him to speak to you, without delay, for a few min-

utes," persisted the waiter, who was doubtless
incited by a large fee.

"Is it a newspaper man?"

"No, sir. More than twenty of these people
have called this morning, but, according to your
orders, we have sent them away."

'A police officer, then?"

"Oh, no, sir! If you would just look at the
card he has sent up."

Young Delorme saw that there was no escape
from this importunity. He rose grumblingly and
took the bit of pasteboard at the door.

Not without astonishment he read:

BARON E. PLÜCKE

*would be greatly obliged to M. Lucien Delorme
if he would see him for a few minutes.*

29, Avenue des Champs-Elysées.

He knew the name. Who, even in the depths
of his province, would have been ignorant of it?
It was no less famous than that of Rothschild.
His fortune, his house, his magnificent collections,
his racing-stables, his generosity in heading all
subscriptions, all works of charity, had made this
millionaire financier a Parisian personage who was
universally famous.

And Baron Plücke had come himself, at this early hour, to request a few minutes' conversation?

Lucien Delorme was filled with mingled pride and anxiety. There must be a very grave reason to induce a person of such importance to give himself so much trouble.

"If he will wait until I have time to dress," he said to the waiter, "I will see him."

"Five minutes later he entered the drawing-room, a regulation family boarding-house drawing-room, with its shabby, incongruous, old-fashioned furniture whose solidity, however, was proof against every ordeal, and which had seen several generations of boarders gaze at the gilt clock on the mantelpiece under its round globe, the terra cotta on the pier tables, and the artificial flowers in the vases.

The baron was waiting patiently.

He was a man about fifty years old, small, but with an air of undeniable distinction and elegance, to whom a long beard thickly mingled with silver threads gave an appearance of impressive importance, emphasized by the little red rosette in his buttonhole.

"Baron Plücke?" asked the young man.

The latter rose, and coming forward, replied:

"Yes, I am Baron Plücke."

45

"You asked for me, sir?"

With a gracious gesture his visitor invited him to take a chair near him.

Then, when both were seated, he began:

"First, I must apologize, sir, for disturbing you in this way, and insisting so urgently upon talking with you. But I beg you not to regard my conduct as mere curiosity, as it might at first appear to you."

Lucien Delorme bowed.

"What is the matter in question?"

"This is the affair. While reading, just now, an account of the terrible drama that occurred in this very house, I was struck by one detail of your story to the chief of the detective service."

"You know that . . ."

Yes, I know that you afterwards declared that it was imaginary, that you had dreamed it, and no attention should be paid to the matter. Nevertheless, I attach to it a value which you will understand when I have related the following facts. Four years ago, my uncle, Baron Plücke-Strohé was murdered in his home in the Avenue d'Antin. One morning he was found in his chamber, with the death-rattle in his throat, which was cut by a steel wire, like Mrs. Tankery's. This similarity of operation is nothing very singular, and might be only a sad coincidence. But this is nothing.

46

Before expiring, my uncle had the strength to stammer a few barely intelligible words: *bullet . . . head . . . leg . . .* The inquest explained the meaning of these three words: near his bed a revolver was found which never left his possession and from which two balls, of which no trace could be found, were missing. So it was easy to infer that my uncle, to defend himself, had fired twice before being disabled by the fatal attack, and that he had shot his assailants in the head and in the leg. Instructions were instantly sent to all the hospitals for descriptions of every individual having a wound of this nature. But, of course, no one went to them. I will add that the criminals were never discovered, and that I vainly offered a reward of a hundred thousand francs to anyone whose information would put me on their trail."

He stopped an instant to take breath, then went on:

"You understand now, sir, that if one of Mrs. Tankery's murderers had a bullet in his skull, the other in the femur, it is very probable that these are the same men who killed my poor uncle."

"That is probable, certainly," replied Lucien Delorme; "but, what can I . . . ."

"What can you do? Why you must see clearly that you hold in your hand the key of the entire mystery. Your words possess decisive weight in my conjectures. The reason I have come to find you is to entreat you to give me all the information that . . ."

"Sir," interrupted the young man coldly, "it is impossible for me to tell you anything more than the newspapers have related of these scoundrels, and, if I answered that I knew nothing, it is the truth."

"And I," cried the baron violently, "I tell you in my turn that you do know something . . . I don't know what . . . I don't know how . . . that is your secret, keep it. But in order not to prolong the discussion uselessly, I will add one thing: I formerly promised a reward of one hundred thousand francs to the person whose information would put me on the track of my uncle's murderers. . . . Well, now I will double the amount; I will offer you two hundred!"

Lucien Delorme had started up suddenly. His face was very pale.

"Do you want to buy me, sir?"

"Why not at all. I need your help. I will pay for it, that's all. Since you have no connection with Mrs. Tankery's murderers, I do not see what scruple should prevent you from accepting my propositions. You place at my service your in-

48

genuity, your keenness of scent, your activity: there is no dishonor in that!"

"But," the young man still objected, "is not the police force better fitted to accomplish such a task successfully than I am?"

"The police will never discover anything. The criminals have taken every precaution to throw them off the trail. As in the Avenue d'Antin, they have done their work with gloves, so as to leave no betraying evidence behind. We must rely solely upon ourselves."

"I had made very different plans. I intended to leave Paris this very day . . . my old mother is expecting me in our home . . ."

But the baron perceived that Delorme's resolution was weakening and that the game was won.

"You will not go!"

"And suppose I should not succeed?" the young man asked, "for, after all, this is my beginning in the trade of detective. . . . I shall have lost my time, not to mention that——"

"Set your mind at rest on that score," interrupted the other, who had not misunderstood the meaning of these words. "From to-day, an apartment will be reserved for you, at my expense, in the Gigantic Palace, Avenue des Champs-Elysées, opposite to my own house. Besides, I shall of course assume all the expenses incurred in your measures—and rest assured that I shall question nothing."

"Yet if, nevertheless . . ."

The baron smiled. It was useless to consider that possibility. He himself felt no doubt. The lure of so large a reward is not to be resisted. He had his man. In a few days the latter would speak.

"Then we are agreed?" the visitor asked more insistently.

Delorme seemed, for an instant, to be still hesitating.

Did the task appear to him to be beyond his powers? Had he any secret reason for refusing to aid in arresting the murderers? Or was he delaying merely to reflect once more upon an event which had caused him so annoying a misadventure?

But suddenly he held out his hand to the baron.

"Very well, sir, you can rely upon me!"

"Thank you!" replied the millionaire. "And, whatever happens, you may be sure of my gratitude."

Delorme bowed.

"When shall you set to work?" Baron Plücke added.

"This very day."

But when he had accompanied his visitor to

the door of the house, Lucien Delorme, as he returned, murmured:

"Here I am a detective. It's a true saying that we never know what life has in store for us. Sherlock Holmes and Nick Carter must look to themselves in future! Two hundred thousand francs are worth taking a little trouble for. Only, I'm entirely ignorant of my new trade: where shall I begin?"

During this monologue he pursued his way to the office:

"Madame Armelin," he said, entering, "will you be kind enough to send for a cab and have my trunk brought down? By the way, I have changed my plans. I shall not leave Paris—and I will ask you to write down my new address, so that my letters can be forwarded."

Then, in a careless tone, he added:

"Gigantic Palace . . . Champs-Elysées."

CHAPTER IV

A PROFITABLE BIT OF BUSINESS

BARON PLÜCKE had not made his fortune solely on the Stock Exchange—a first-class business man, no branch of speculation was unfamiliar to him, and for thirty years he had been interested in all the great enterprises which had enriched their stockholders.

A bachelor, a multimillionaire, able to indulge, without hesitation, his most costly fancies, people wondered why he still devoted himself to work.

It was purely from inclination. Baron Plücke could not be idle.

Every morning he received everyone who came to his office. He listened to them patiently, took notes and, a few days later, his secretary wrote his decisions concerning their proposals or their requests, for petitioners, as may be supposed, were no less numerous than inventors.

Besides, no man lived more simply than he.

Though he owned a gallery of wonderful pictures, where all the schools of painting were represented by masterpieces, though his racing stable

52

was famous as one of the most magnificent in the world, though his name appeared heading the subscriptions of every club, every art exhibition, every charitable society and pleasure meeting of Parisian life, he himself had no luxury. A single valet gave all the service he required, and people would have been astonished if they had entered his home at meal hours to see the frugality of his table, or to meet him, after leaving his automobile at the garage, pursuing his way, like the most modest citizen, on foot or in an autobus.

On the very day of his interview with Lucien Delorme, at Madame Armelin's family boardinghouse, his valet, on his return, gave him the card of a visitor who had been waiting several moments:

COMTE D'ABAZOLI-VISCOSA

Ex Embassy Attaché
Representing

His Highness the Maharajah of Pandhukurrah
4, Rue Vézelay.

The baron knew his caller, having met him already several times in society, where a mutual friend had introduced them to each other.

He gave orders that he should be admitted at once.

53

The visitor was a man still young in appearance, distinguished in bearing, with pleasant features, keen eyes, and a slightly bronzed complexion, being a native of Sicily, where his relatives had perished in the terrible earthquake that destroyed Messina.

Baron Plücke shook hands with him, invited him to a seat, and courteously asked the reason for his visit.

"You are not ignorant, sir," replied the comte, "that I am the Paris representative of the Maharajah of Pandhukurrah. It would be too long a story, and moreover useless, to explain why I left the diplomatic career to occupy this position. I will tell you simply that I have succeeded my father, who himself owed it to the deep affection of the prince, whose life he had saved in a tiger hunt. His Highness desired to transfer to me the confidence he reposed in him. But," he interrupted himself, "this has nothing to do with the object of my visit, and I will go to the point . . ."

The Maharajah of Pandhukurrah, of whom Comte d'Abazoli-Viscosa spoke, was—if rumor could be credited—one of the richest and most powerful of the Indian princes. He owned immense territories, superb palaces, elephants and bayaderes by thousands, and endless wealth.

When he went out on an elephant caparisoned

with gold brocade embroidered with pearls, its tusks adorned with chased rings, a throng of horsemen, in brilliant uniforms, pranced around him on spirited steeds, bearing as weapons damascened guns and sabers incrusted with precious stones.

Nothing could equal his wonderful entertainments except those described in the *Arabian Nights,* and when he arranged a hunting party he took with him a regular army of elephant drivers, beaters, grass cutters, tent-raisers, palanquin bearers, cooks, and servants of all kinds.

It would seem that a life so luxurious must flow on forever amid the roses of the Persian poet; his pride, unfortunately, planted thorns among these.

It will be remembered that, at the Durbar of Delhi where, according to custom, the English king received the homage of all the Hindoo princes, one alone among them refused to kneel and kiss the ground before the new emperor.

This was the Maharajah of Pandhukurrah.

Going forward to the foot of the throne, he bowed deferentially, and retired in the same way, considering his lineage too noble for him to make before another man those signs of reverence due only to Buddha.

The English government, though deeply irritated by this attitude, made no comment; but it was certain that at the first opportunity it would dethrone and exile a prince who gave his people, ever ready to revolt against their ancient oppressor, so haughty a lesson of independence.

This was a fact of which the Maharajah could not be ignorant.

So, foreseeing the future awaiting him, he occupied himself in prudently placing a portion of his wealth where it would be secure, depositing part of it in European banks, and giving a portion to some loyal friends, so that he could easily get possession of it in time of need.

In this way Comte d'Abazoli-Viscosa, the father of the man who was talking with Baron Plücke, received in charge his marvelous jewels, a trust which the son inherited a few years later, after the catastrophe of Messina.

All this was known by everyone in Paris and, in relating it, the young man was telling the baron nothing new.

"Many things have occurred since that time," the visitor continued. "The Maharajah has really been dispossessed. But he has obtained permission to live on in his palace under the rigid surveillance of the British government, and to retain his wealth. Now he finds that he needs for an enterprise concerning which I am required to maintain absolute secrecy and which, as you suspect, concerns politics exclusively, a very large sum of money. He cannot collect the amount in India without attracting the attention of his jailers. So he thought it would be easy for him to borrow it in Europe by giving first-class security: his jewels. This, sir, is the transaction I have come to propose to you."

Baron Plücke, who had listened in silence, reflected an instant.

"How much is wanted?" he asked.

"Fifteen millions."

"And what is the estimated value of the prince's jewels?"

"About fifty."

"Where are they now?"

"At my residence, in my safe. This is done to have them constantly at hand and avoid all the formalities of depositing them in a bank, which might delay a prompt withdrawal."

"For what length of time would this loan be needed?"

"A year."

"And the rate of interest?"

"This is the plan. To avoid any discussion on the subject of interest, I am commissioned to make you this offer: our agreement will be for twenty millions, and you will give us only fifteen. That, you see, is a good rate of interest."

The baron, who was taking notes, raised his head and, looking intently at the speaker, said:

"And what proof do you give me that you are authorized to treat in the name of the Maharajah of Pandhukurrah?"

"The best. The money will be paid by you directly to His Highness through a French bank in Pondichery or Karikal. At first there was talk of a journey, during which it would have been easy to negotiate directly. The government, through a system of petty annoyance, would not authorize him to leave India. I am ready to give you the autograph letter in which he asks me to negotiate this transaction in person, but it seems to me that the prince's receipt on the checks will be the best proof of his consent!"

Then, as the baron nodded assent, he continued:

"Perhaps it might be advisable that you should first see the jewels, and have an expert estimate their value?"

The baron, with a wave of his hand, signified that there was no occasion for anyone's assistance, he would attend to the matter himself.

"Under those circumstances," said the comte, "the transaction is still more simple! As His Highness desires the utmost caution and the greatest possible haste, you might appoint a meeting at any day and hour that suits your convenience, examine the jewels and, when the contract is signed, take them away at once, for," he added smiling, "I shall be glad to be relieved as soon as possible from the responsibility of such a fortune! As to the rest, you will only have to send the money to the prince and I feel no anxiety on that subject."

Baron Plücke, opening a cigarette case, offered it to his guest, and having lighted his own and taken a few whiffs, answered:

"On first thought, Comte, I should be rather inclined to undertake this affair. The sum is rather large. Fifteen millions! But I think it will be easy to raise it with the aid of a few friends. A transaction of this kind is financed like a factory or a mine. Yet, before reaching any decision, I must examine it in detail and make a few inquiries."

"That is perfectly fair. I will add that it will be formally stated in the contract that if, through any accident, the prince should fail to make his payments on the date named, you would have the absolute right to protect yourself by the sale of the security. So you will incur no risk in a deal that is perfectly honest on both sides."

"Very good. You shall have your answer in a few days. Will you be kind enough to call in again next week?"

"Certainly."

The baron was just rising when a final question fell from his caller's lips:

"We have forgotten something—the usual little commission . . . ?"

"Oh yes. Please tell me how much you want for managing the matter."

"A million."

"A million!" cried the startled baron.

"Is the price excessive?" replied the other coldly. "Don't forget that in a year, without the slightest risk, I am helping you make four."

"Of course, but a million for commission! . . ."

"You are at liberty to accept or refuse. I came to you, sir, because I knew you to be a man with whom one can reach an understanding. But, since the transaction doesn't suit you on the terms I offer, I will go elsewhere. The proposition is good enough for me to have no trouble in making the arrangement!"

The baron appeared to hesitate an instant, then he answered abruptly:

"Since you require it, I shall be compelled to submit to your terms, but allow me to tell you that you are an extremely expensive agent!"

"Pshaw!" replied the comte, "business is business. . . . The only person who might have reason to complain of all these combinations is His

60

Highness! And, in connection with this, I must inform you that there is one point upon which I absolutely insist: no one must know of this affair. You perceive the injury it might do me with His Highness, if it should ever reach his ears. So I must request, sir, that as soon as the contract is signed and the jewels are in your possession, you will give me this sum from hand to hand, in bank notes, without requiring any receipt. . . ."

"Why is——"

"I make it an absolute condition. This is my only way of being sure that no proof will exist against me in this matter, and that the entire transaction will always remain a secret between ourselves."

"Very well, sir," assented the baron, who was accustomed to these kinds of combinations. "In case the business is concluded, the money shall be paid in the way you require. I will make the promise."

He accompanied him to the door and, with a last clasp of the hands, the two men separated, with a mutual:

"Hope to see you again soon!"

While Baron Plücke was studying the proposition which the representative of the Maharajah of Pandhukurrah had come to make him, Lucien Delorme, settled at the Gigantic Palace, was reflecting, with his head between his hands, upon the means of finding Mrs. Tankery's murderers.

A week had passed without his discovering any clue.

If the newspapers would only put him on some trail! But they remained silent. For lack of elements to satisfy, daily, the curiosity of their readers, they had gradually forgotten the drama which, for a time, had caused so deep an interest. Other miscellaneous items of news had since aroused the attention of the public. *The Crime of the Faubourg Saint-Denis, The Mystery of the Boulevard Malesherbes, The Disappearance of the Rue de Rennes.*

As for the murderer of the Rue Mozart, the investigation had not made one step in advance since the Chief of the Detective Bureau had officially declared that "the crime was signed" and that it was "professional."

If the police, with all the means at its disposal, is powerless, thought the young man sorrowfully, what can I do? How does it help me to be certain, against the whole world, though M. Clamart said that I was under a hallucination, and the entire press treated me as if I were a lunatic, to be certain, I repeat, that the taller of the two murderers has a bullet in his head, and the other in his leg! How am I to discover these two individuals among the millions of the inhabitants of Paris? To do so would require a singular accident! Like taking a lottery ticket with the expectation of winning the great prize. No, no, I am really stealing Baron Plücke's money, that's all . . . and comfortable as I am in this superb hotel, I am going to tell him that I refuse to continue this profession of detective, for which I have no aptitude, and prefer to return to Eu, where my mother is begging me to join her.

With these words, he took his hat and, with a firm step, crossing the Avenue des Champs-Elysées, went up to the baron's office.

"Anybody but me would profit by this situation. For a week, not once have I set foot outside the door! With the means at my command, I might know something about the fashionable life of Paris, and . . ."

But he interrupted himself and, with drooping head, added in a tone of sorrowful discouragement:

"What's the use?"

He rang the bell. When his name was announced, the baron requested him to wait a few minutes. He was engaged just then with Comte d'Abazoli-Viscosa. He had decided to conclude the arrangement. If the Maharajah's jewels possessed the value attributed to them, the security of the loan was assured. As for the comte, he had the reputation of being a man of honor, full of devotion to the Hindoo prince whom he represented. Under these circumstances, Baron Plücke had easily obtained from his friends the fifteen millions wanted, and was explaining the details to the comte, whom he had summoned.

"Day after to-morrow, at three o'clock," he said in conclusion, "I will go to your residence." Then, handing him a paper, he added: "Meanwhile, will you read this outline of the contract?"

The other took the document and read it slowly, seeming to weigh each word.

"That is excellent. I will ask only that you will have three copies, one for yourself, one which I shall send to His Highness, and one to keep among my accounts. . . ."

While the baron was writing this request in his notebook, for his secretary, the comte added:

"The jewels will be at your disposal; do you intend to take them at once?"

"Wasn't that agreed?" asked the baron quickly.

"As soon as our signatures are exchanged, you can dispose of them as you choose. I spoke of it in case you might wish to have them taken by some confidential man."

"No. I'll bring a small valise with me, and shall trust the matter to no one."

"And you are not afraid that . . ."

"That is my usual method. Why should I attract attention by unusual precautions? There are always robbers on the watch who would think: 'Come, come, Baron Plücke has just done a good piece of business, let's hold him up.' That would be laying myself open uselessly to their attacks! So, with my valise, I'll just step into the first cab that comes along, as if I were merely attending to some ordinary matter."

"Won't you at least allow me to send my valet with you? He'll ride on the box."

"No indeed. On leaving your home, I shall go directly to the Bank of France and the jewels will be immediately deposited in my safe, without letting anyone suspect that Baron Plücke has crossed all Paris with fifty millions on his person!"

"After all, you are right," replied the comte.

"Oh, I assure you that having such a fortune in my house has often kept me from sleeping! What wouldn't I have given if people had not known it! But to try to hide anything from that Argus of a hundred eyes whose name is Paris!—One would think that the walls themselves had ears."

While speaking, he had risen:

"Day after to-morrow, then, sir." Lowering his voice, he added: "By the way, I thought that, for my commission, I would willingly accept a check

65

made out to bearer, if that would suit your convenience better."

"No, no," answered the baron, patting him familiarly on the shoulder, "what is agreed is agreed."

He accompanied him to the door, passing through the drawing-room.

Lucien Delorme was waiting patiently to be admitted, meanwhile admiring the magnificent tapestries hung on the walls which, in a famous sale, the baron had torn from America with volleys of bank-notes.

He had pushed his immovable black glasses up on his forehead, and was examining *Jupiter Abducting Europa*, famed throughout the whole world of collectors, which experts agreed in considering the finest Gobelin in existence when, suddenly, the door opened and the two men appeared.

Absorbed in their conversation, they crossed the immense apartment without noticing the young man in his corner, who had mechanically glanced toward them.

Suddenly he started, seemed to fix his whole attention on them, and gazed with a keen expression until they had disappeared.

Then, passing his hand across his forehead with a feverish gesture, he murmured:

"It is impossible!"

66

Just at that moment the baron came toward him, exclaiming cordially:

"Ah, Monsieur Delorme, I am glad to see you!"

Then, while ushering him into his private office, he asked:

"Well, have you found anything interesting?"

"Perhaps so," replied the young man slowly.

"And it is . . . ?"

"Don't ask me anything yet. Allow me to-day to put a few questions."

And as the other assented, he said:

"Who is the man from whom you just parted?"

The baron looked at him with a little astonishment.

"Comte d'Abazoli-Viscosa," he replied.

"One of your friends?"

"No, the representative of a Hindoo prince, with whom I am doing some business."

In a few rapid words he informed Delorme of the transaction he intended to carry out, and the meeting which he had appointed for the next day but one, with the comte.

"Do you know anything discreditable to him?" he added.

"This is the first time I ever heard of him. Only there is an old proverb that says all roads lead to Rome, yet we must not, on that account, neglect anything that can put us on the right one. But, sir, in a few days I shall doubtless have some news for you. That is what I came to tell you this morning."

While going down the staircase, he muttered in a low tone:

"Oh, chance—chance, yes, the ancients had good reason to invoke it. Who would have said that, while going to the baron to inform him that I would give up trying to discover the murderers of the Avenue Mozart, I should leave him with hope?"

CHAPTER V

COMTE D'ABAZOLI-VISCOSA was right in saying that in Paris everything was known. In fact, no one was ignorant that he was the guardian of a part of the treasures of the Maharajah of Pandhukurrah.

In the drawing-rooms of the fashionable circles he frequented, the fame of having in his residence fifty millions of jewels gave him the little halo which surrounds persons of note, and attracted attention, in a very flattering manner, to the handsome, agreeable, distinguished looking fellow.

Weary of evading all the questions asked concerning the wonderful gems, he had finally yielded, without too much urging, gave a description of the splendor of these marvels, worthy of an Oriental tale, and did not even refuse to permit the most curious inquirers to see the safe in his home which contained them, an iron-cased chest nearly two yards high, closed by a large number of impregnable locks. So, in spite of what he had

69

told Baron Plücke, the comte could sleep quietly without fear of burglars.

But when he was asked to allow just a glimpse, if it were only for an instant, of these famous jewels, he drew back, smiling, behind the professional discretion to which he was pledged.

"There are only two persons who know the secret of the safe," he replied: "His Highness and myself. So, whatever desire I may have to oblige you, it is evident that I cannot use it without his formal authorization."

This was speaking like an honest man and it was useless to insist.

But it was not only in fashionable society that this enormous fortune aroused legitimate curiosity; it had excited the greed also of the world of thieves.

More than one robber, on the watch for some profitable job, had thought of getting possession of it; but hitherto, the most skillful, as well as the boldest, had failed: the safe had remained inviolable, and the Hindoo servant placed by the prince at the service of his representative who, every evening slept in the room where it stood, had discovered the criminals even before they had had time to reach him.

So the report had gradually spread among them that there was nothing to be done in that

70

quarter, and that the Rajah's well-guarded jewels must be let alone.

Yet all had not utterly determined to give up this fine booty, and so some were still waiting, with tireless patience, a favorable moment to make an attempt.

Among their number was the "A" band. What was the meaning of the name? Were they the Apaches, the Aristos, or the Aminches of some distant Belleville or vague Grenelle?

An Œdipus would probably have lost his way in seeking the etymology, yet nothing was more simple than the truth.

The three scoundrels who had united to pillage, in partnership, the property of others, had noticed that, through a singular coincidence, their Christian names commenced with the same letter, the first of the alphabet.

From that day they called themselves the "A's."

These, however, were no ordinary criminals, knights of the knife, assailants of drunkards or watchers for belated pedestrians; their aims were higher. They attempted only certain and productive operations, and their feats were perplexing through the cleverness with which they were planned and executed.

There was the jewelry shop in the Boulevard

71

Sebastopol, rifled one night by burglars who had entered through the cellar, cutting a hole in the floor, and retired with their booty without permitting the proprietor, who slept on the floor above, to hear the least sound; the safe in the Turco-Italian bank, which between two rounds of watchmen, was blown up with dynamite; and in the provinces, the theft of the treasure of the Cathedral of Caen, carried off in broad daylight by masked bandits, in an automobile, unseen by anyone.

All these and many other exploits, no less audacious, were the work of the "A" band.

These three men, besides, completed one another marvelously, uniting the qualities indispensable to the dangerous trade they pursued, one contributing to the partnership his strength, the second his skill, the third his intuition.

The first, Alphonse, an ex-wrestler, was a sort of Colossus, capable of bursting open the strongest door with a thrust of his shoulder, of twisting a bar of iron between his fingers like a wisp of straw, and of coping with four determined men.

Augustus, the second, formerly a locksmith, possessed incredible dexterity, peerless ingenuity. He found means of baffling the closest watch, of entering easily the best defended places, and of setting at defiance the most complicated locks, making, when necessary, all the tools required.

As for the third man, Anatole, a short, slender fellow, with pleasing features, whose beardless face made him appear still very young, his specialty was to disguise himself as a woman. And this he did with so much skill, such perfect naturalness, that it was impossible to help being deceived.

In the hotels, casinos, and certain classes of society where the company was a little mixed and very accessible, his aid was especially valuable. Playing carelessly with his fan, he listened to what was said about him, and turned the information thus obtained to his profit. Who would even have thought of suspecting so agreeable and charming a woman of being the accomplice of the criminals who, during the night had rifled the apartment of a wealthy customer of the Palace or robbed a villa when its occupants were at the Casino? Besides, he was an admirable connoisseur, peerless in selling stolen jewels and getting rid, through unscrupulous receivers, of the valuable artistic property that fell into his hands.

So each one had his clearly defined place in the band, and it was not surprising that, with so perfect an organization, it was prosperous and safe from surprises.

It may be supposed that Anatole had not been long in hearing of the existence of the Maharajah's jewels, and that, since then, the whole attention of his colleagues had been turned in their direction.

But how were they to conquer the almost insurmountable difficulties that must be overcome, how were they even to reach the magic treasure?

Not a day passed without the discussion of this question among them and the forming of some new plan.

Beneath the costume of Lady Dufferton, Anatole had succeeded one day in getting himself included among the guests to whom the comte had shown the famous safe.

He had received the impression that the task was impossible to attempt.

"I suppose," he concluded, "that after getting rid, in some way, of the Hindoo who sleeps before the safe, we could reach it, but how shall we open it? To force its numerous locks is a tremendous labor which could not be done in a single night!"

"And where does it stand?" suddenly asked Augustus, who had listened a few moments in silence.

"In the comte's office."

"Is that in the apartment?"

"The last room on the front—at the end of the

74

passage—two windows . . . four yards to five-fifty," he added, with the positiveness of a man whose swift observation is infallible.

"Then it would be against the next house?"

"Certainly."

"And is that like the one the comte occupies?"

"The construction is precisely the same—built by the same architect. I happened to notice it in looking at the numbers."

"Well. . . ."

He reflected an instant, and then inquired:

"Against which wall does the safe stand?"

"Against the division wall of the next house."

"In which corner?"

Anatole collected his memories.

"On the left as you enter—that is, at the back of the room."

"Well, my friends," said Augustus slowly, "the Rajah's jewels are ours."

The two men uttered the same exclamation in one breath:

"How is that?"

Augustus, in a few swift words, explained his plan:

"Oh, I can take no great credit for discovering it. Chance favors us, that's all. Listen! I think, from what Anatole says, that any daring attempt to steal this treasure would be useless; it is well guarded. But suppose that there should be a vacant apartment in the house next to the one occupied by Comte d'Abazoli-Viscosa, an apartment also on the ground floor, that is, adjoining his own. Who can prevent our hiring it and moving in?"

"Nobody," cried the giant, who was trying to understand what the speaker was driving at.

"Then," his colleague went on, "after having carefully marked the exact position of the safe, we must pierce the wall without letting anyone suspect what we are doing and get to the safe itself. After that we need only wait till the comte is away, for he leaves Paris sometimes, doesn't he?"

"Yes," replied Anatole, "he has a villa at Cabourg, where he often goes to rest for a day or two."

"Well, during this time, having no cause to fear that the safe may be suddenly opened while we are working on it . . ."

"The comte," interrupted Anatole, "said in my presence, that he would never do it without a formal order from the prince."

"And why shouldn't the order reach him at that precise moment? Don't laugh. Stranger coincidences than that have been witnessed! One must anticipate everything. I'll go on. Then we will make an opening in the back of the safe by means of oxyhydrogen pipes, and take possession of the Maharajah's gems without letting the vigilant watchman on duty on the other side perceive anything wrong."

"On condition, however," remarked the colossus, "that your blow pipes are powerful enough."

"Don't worry about that, my dear fellow!" retorted Augustus, winking. "We will cut that steel, no matter how solid it may be, as easily as a ball of butter. Besides, we're not afraid of a wall of rubble an inch thick, are we?"

"No!"

"Then, my friends, what do you say to my plan?"

"Wonderful!" cried the two men.

"I see but one objection," the young man continued, "and that has no connection with the method of proceeding, which seems to me very ingenious."

"Speak, Brother."

"In the first place, the apartment adjoining the comte's must be vacant. But it isn't. There is nothing for rent in either of the houses. And if the tenant, on whose departure we are depending, should renew his lease for three, six, or nine months, the Maharajah will have time to resume possession of his famous jewels before we can advance any farther than we are now!"

"We shall know our chances to-morrow. Janitors don't have tongues without being able to use them. But, before going any farther, there is an important question to be considered. This business will be expensive to manage. I want to warn you of that. The apartment, the furniture— perhaps one or two years of waiting. All that time the money will slip away! You'll have to use all your means, and go to the bottom of your savings. Do you feel courageous enough to do it?"

Then, as the other two nodded assent, he persisted:

"Think it over carefully; we shall have to sow heavily before we reap!"

But the giant abruptly declared:

"I'm ready. I have confidence. I believe that we shall succeed. And fifty millions is a sum worth while. It deserves risking a few thousand to win."

"But suppose we should fail?" said Anatole, who was less enthusiastic. "Think of the difficulties before us."

"No matter what comes!" replied the other. "Whenever I start on an expedition, I say to myself: 'Old man, you may wind up at Cayenne.'

This time I shall think: 'Perhaps it is your goose that's going to be cooked!' That's all!"

"Without reckoning that this won't save you from Cayenne!"

"Don't bring us bad luck, Anatole!" exclaimed the giant angrily, hastily touching wood to avert the evil fate. "Those things come themselves without being summoned! Come, Augustus, make out your account, so that we may see whether we can become your stockholders. How much do you want?"

Taking a pencil and paper, Augustus began his calculations.

But it was written that fortune should decidedly favor the "A" band.

Three months after this conversation, the apartment which they coveted was made vacant by the tenant's sudden death.

They were informed the very next morning and, a few days after, moving vans stopped before the house with the furniture of the new occupants, a foreigner who had recently arrived in Paris and settled there with his two servants.

As he had asked for no repairs, had not discussed the amount of the rent, paid for the quarter in advance, and been very generous in the deposit money, no further inquiries had been made.

The Rue Vézelay is a particularly quiet street

which in this pretty quarter of the VIIIe ward, seems to have retained a provincial atmosphere. Private residences, more numerous than the apartment houses, huge caravanserais that have gradually invaded Paris, permit glimpses of the green foliage in their little gardens. Carriages rarely pass, there are no shops, and no noises of crowds disturb its placid stillness.

The arrival of the new resident was wholly unnoticed.

It was not the same with his servants, a big cook with shoulders of athletic breadth, and a young groom who, by a singular antithesis, was slender and delicate. Their cheerful humor, their gift of the gab, their readiness in telling tales of their stirring life in the service of an eccentric master, were speedily appreciated in the neighborhood, and they had not been settled a month before they were intimate with all of the same class in both of the two adjoining houses, and were not ignorant of any gossip in the whole street.

Only the servants of Comte d'Abazoli-Viscosa, who held aloof and associated with no one, had ignored all their advances. One was the famous Hindoo, who acted as cook, butler, and chauffeur, and the other, a maid, a tall, handsome dark girl, who did not even condescend, when she passed the janitor's room, to stop for a little chat.

"Attitudinisers!" said the janitress. "They think it's a great thing to live with a Maharajah's ambassador! But talking with people a bit wouldn't make them steal his jewels."

"Of course not!" the big cook answered.

And by dwelling skillfully on this subject, so important to him, he had obtained all the information he desired concerning the habits of her tenant.

Meanwhile, the three accomplices had set to work in the apartment.

Stone by stone, with slow patience, they toiled to break through the wall to reach the safe. In this delicate task they were past masters. Not a sound had attracted the attention of the neighbors. They worked in silence, with consummate skill.

Each day they rid themselves of the materials removed, and carefully cleared away every external sign of their labor, in the fear of an ever possible surprise.

The safe was soon reached. Nothing remained except to enlarge the almost invisible hole, which was the affair of scarcely a few hours.

They now needed merely to wait for the favorable moment. June had come. This was the time when the comte would probably leave to go to his villa on the seashore.

The last preparations were completed, the

oxyhydrogen pipes made and all the details of an immediate flight to England studied.

It was probable that the robbery would not be discovered before the return of the comte, and that they would have all the time required to disappear. But it was none the less necessary to take every useful precaution, and it was agreed that each should go by himself in a roundabout way, and disguised.

At last, one evening, Alphonse brought his companions a piece of sensational news.

It was the day after the comte's last visit to Baron Plücke, during which they had come to an agreement about the loan of twenty millions.

The comte had told the janitor that he expected to leave Paris the next day, taking his servants with him.

"Imprudent fellow!" cried Augustus. "My friends, we have the Maharajah's jewels!"

CHAPTER VI

A WELL-CONTRIVED CRIME

AFTER leaving Baron Plücke's, the comte
went directly home.

"Has anyone called on me, Nam?"

"No, M. le Comte, no one," replied the servant.

He was a little brown-skinned man, of uncertain
age, who wore the costume usual among the servants of his country, a white waistcloth and
jacket, with a red and yellow silk handkerchief
wound around his head. His keen little eyes and
odd gestures made him resemble a fakir or a serpent charmer.

The Maharajah himself had sent this man to
the former Comte d'Abazoli-Viscosa and, on the
latter's death, his son had retained the Hindoo in
his service.

The comte willingly allowed it to be understood
that he suspected the man of watching him discreetly in behalf of the prince. But, he added, he
was so devoted, so attentive, so honest, that he
had decided to pretend ignorance. At any rate,
he was of great value to him in reading the Maha-

rajah's letters, which were all written in Hindustani, not a word of which did he know, and he would have been most reluctant to trust to a stranger.

"Is there anything I can do for M. le Comte?"

"Not just now, Nam. I'll ring presently. Has Juliette returned?"

"She is at work in the linen room."

"Very well."

The comte, crossing the passage, crammed with all the trifles he had brought back from his journeys to India, entered his office, a very plain room, as was appropriate, with the immense safe, its large desk, its imposing bookcases, and its dark hangings.

He looked at himself in the glass a moment and, slowly passing his fingers through his jet black hair, uttered a sigh of satisfaction. He was evidently pleased with himself and had succeeded in accomplishing what he desired.

Then, going to the mantelpiece, he pressed the bell-button once, twice.

A minute later the door opened and Nam and Juliette appeared. But, at sight of them, the comte instantly dropped his lordly air and, in a tone of entire familiarity exclaimed, rapping on the table:

"Well, it's done!"

"Going on well?" asked the Hindoo, also suddenly abandoning his manner of a well-trained servant.

"Day after to-morrow, at three o'clock, he will be here to examine the jewels, with the little million for the commission in his pocket!"

"And," questioned the Hindoo, "does he come alone?"

"Entirely alone! Things have turned out even better than I expected. He'll bring a small valise . . ."

"Well planned!"

"So we have nothing more to do except make all the necessary arrangements not to fail in our job. Oh, my good Nam," he added, throwing up his arms, "I long at last to have the fortune! For ten years we have lived, day after day, on expedients and expeditions, with the perpetual fear of being pinched. I shouldn't be sorry to retire!"

"Pshaw!" replied the other: "the trade has risks, it's true! But wouldn't you prefer to lead the pleasant life of a society man rather than have remained a poor little bailiff's clerk in the depths of a province? For my part, don't you think I am better off to be a servant in a good house than a breaker up of boats on the wharves of Marseilles? Whatever may happen to you in the future, you've had ten years of comfort. Life is short. We must enjoy it!"

"Yes. You certainly had a bright idea when you invented the Maharajah and his jewels. It gives us unlimited credit everywhere. We owe all the good shops. The rest are only waiting for our orders! Nevertheless, there are days when I feel strangely weary of playing this part and long for peace of mind. I assure you that if we hadn't found this usurer Plücke and his million, I would have sent my countship and the Maharajah to the deuce and dropped everything!"

"You know very well that that wouldn't have been possible! You will now remain all your life Comte d'Abazoli-Viscosa. I had trouble enough in manufacturing your official papers!"

"Granted! But when, in consequence of the events of which we shall talk presently, His Highness has withdrawn his confidence, I shall be able to disappear from Parisian society and live as a gentleman-farmer in some quiet corner and devote myself to agriculture and breeding. At heart, you see, I have always had rural tastes,—I dream of . . . But," he interrupted himself, "this isn't the time to discuss such questions! Let us attend to figures. How much is our floating debt?"

"Do you mean to settle it?"

"I consider that absolutely necessary, Nam. We must go without leaving anything connected with the past behind us. Some day it might create useless trouble."

"Agreed. About two hundred thousand francs . . . ."

"As much as that?" cried the comte in surprise. "What has become of the eighty thousand francs from the Bank of Hayti last year?"

The Hindoo began to laugh:

"You have the soul of a born gentleman! You spend without reckoning, and then ask where the money has gone! Oh!" he went on, "I'm not reproaching you for anything. When a position is to be maintained, the necessary sacrifices must be made!"

"I'll put up two hundred then—and how much of the million do you want for your share?"

"The same amount. I'm not exacting, am I?"

"It's a fortune in your country! You will buy an immense concession and raise rice on a tremendous scale. In ten years you will have ten times the sum!"

"The only misfortune is that I might not go back there."

"Why?" asked the young girl who, until then, had remained silent.

But Nam undoubtedly had reasons which he

considered it prudent to keep to himself, for his eyes wandered and he answered vaguely:

"Political causes . . ."

"There will be six hundred thousand francs left for Juliette and me," said the comte. "At four per cent. that will give an income of eighty thousand francs. But we are reasonable, aren't we, Juliette?"

She threw herself into his arms:

"Since we love each other, shall we not always have enough?"

"Come, come," cried Nam, "no idyls just now! There are more urgent matters to be discussed! The great affair is to come off day after to-morrow. We must examine carefully to see that there is no important point we may have overlooked!"

"Nam," said the comte, "it's fearfully hot to-day: could you give us something to drink?"

The Hindoo bowed very low:

"I'll make M. le Comte a cocktail, the receipt of which was given to me by His Highness himself."

A few minutes after all three were seated before iced drinks and, while drawing his through a long yellow straw, Nam began:

"This is the theme of the maneuver—don't let the expression surprise you," he cried, laughing. "I was once a Sepoy! . . ."

He went on:

"Granting that Baron Plücke will come here, alone, with a little valise to carry to the Bank of France jewels that have no existence, and with a million in his pocket, the point in question is: (1) to seize the million, (2) to provide a proof that he left this apartment with the jewels, (3) during the trip from this house to the bank to do away with him forever and in such a manner that it would be impossible to have any suspicion rest upon us."

"Well stated," said the comte; "we really ought to appear the persons most affected by the robbery. In my opinion, the first operation presents no difficulty. The baron comes here. I show him the safe. He steps forward mechanically to look at it. At that moment, Nam comes out of his usual hiding place, behind that curtain, and . . ."

Then, with a gesture indicating that the steel wire would perform its office:

"The million is ours," he added.

"Capital," answered Nam, without moving a muscle at the thought of the crime he was to commit in so cowardly a manner.

"Let us go on to chapter two. I think the best proof—perhaps the only one—of the delivery of the jewels is the signature on the contract and a

89

receipt proving their delivery into the baron's hands."

"Have you a specimen of his handwriting?"

"I have kept the letter in which he requested me to come to his house yesterday."

"Well, to-morrow you shall have your receipt, written with the same ink and the same pen. Oh," he added modestly, "I have a natural gift for imitating handwritings. As for the contract, five minutes after it is in his note-case, it will be well and duly signed!"

"Your hand will not tremble?"

"It never trembles. Now for chapter three. That is the hardest! The body is lying in this room—the million is in the safe. What shall we do next?"

"Speak, Nam!" said Juliette, breathless from curiosity.

"Next? We'll take off his clothes and, in a jiffy, I'll put them on; you know that my figure is almost exactly like the baron's! As to the rest, everything will be ready, wig, beard, to make me resemble him. I'll defy you to discover any difference! I might have made my fortune by giving imitations of people in the music halls!"

"I'm not uneasy, Nam," said the comte. "You haven't your equal for knowing how to make up! I remember the day you went to cash that check for eighty thousand francs at the Société Générale, as the agent of the bank of Hayti. The cashier knew him well, yet let himself be taken in. You had imitated even his nervous twitching."

"I'll go on. So I leave here in the clothes and with the appearance of Baron Plücke. I go down stairs with my little valise. While passing the janitress's room, I take care to say a few words to her, that she may remember, later, having seen me leave the house. I jump into the cab which is waiting for me, or I call one: 'Driver, to the Bank of France!' On the way, I change my mind: 'Driver, turn round, I want to stop a minute at the Grand Marché.' I go in. The crowd is dense. It is hard to move about. The White Sale is going on. I skillfully take off my beard, my rosette, and if I can, my wig. I hide the little valise under my overcoat. Thus altered, I go out through another door. Don't worry, the cabdriver, who has been waiting till nightfall, will not have forgotten me, and his evidence at the police station will be the best of alibis!"

"Cleverly planned!" assented the comte. "The baron having left here, there is no reason to suspect us. Our threshold once crossed, we are no longer responsible, are we? He had only to accept my offer to let my valet accompany him on the box with the coachman!"

"And the real baron, while all this is going on?" questioned Juliette.

"It won't be very difficult to get rid of him. At midnight, I'll bring up in front of the house the auto carefully disguised, with its number altered. To put a body through a ground floor window into the carriage is mere child's play for us three. The street, as usual, will be deserted."

"And suppose we should be seen? There is a gas jet directly opposite to the house."

"Don't worry. It will be put out, and the darkness will be intense.

"We shall have replaced the baron's clothes, restored his note-case with the signed contract inside, and his valise. Then, on reaching a secluded alley in the Bois de Vincennes, we will quickly get rid of everything, and shall merely have to return to Paris by another way in the auto, which has been restored to its usual appearance, and re-numbered, a little farther on. The next morning the baron's body will be found in the thicket, with his empty valise by his side, and there will be no doubt that he has been lured into some ambush and robbed. What could be more common?" he concluded, laughing.

"And I shall no longer have the responsibility of those fifty millions of gems!" chuckled the comte.

"But, by way of compensation, we shall possess the large sum honestly earned by the sweat of our brow. Well, my friends, I think I have forgotten nothing?"

"No," answered the comte, "I see nothing but chance that could make us fail. And, in that case, look out for our lives."

"Pooh!" retorted the other philosophically, "nothing venture, nothing have!—But what do you expect will happen to us?—Is not everything mathematically combined? I'll answer for the whole affair!"

"Well, let come what may! And next morning I propose that we start for the seashore to enjoy a well-earned rest. A fashionable man, like myself, ought not to stay longer in Paris. It's more than ten days since the Grand Prix."

"Let's be off to the sea then. But on condition that our departure shall appear natural!"

"Why shouldn't it seem so? I have waited for the conclusion of an important business matter . . . as soon as it is settled, I'm off. But never mind, whatever it may be, I shall inform the janitress without appearing to make any point of doing so."

"Then," added the Hindoo, "all this will aid in making the elegant departure you desired. Made desperate by the robbery of the jewels in your charge, but for which, nevertheless, you were not responsible, you send in your resignation to the Maharajah, who accepts it—and, disgusted, you retire from Parisian life . . ."

"And go to live in the country, where I shall marry Juliette . . ."

"Oh," cried the girl, her eyes sparkling with joy, "how happy we shall be!"

"That poor Maharajah is the one who suffers in all this," said Nam. "He is robbed of his fifty millions of jewels . . . he doesn't get the fifteen millions he borrowed either . . . luckily, he is rich enough to bear such a blow!"

While speaking, Nam had drawn a silver bottle from the pail of ice.

"Will Monsieur le Comte have a little of the cocktail?"

"Yes, Nam!"

Then, raising his glass:

"To the success of the plan for day after to-morrow!" he cried, and touching his glass to Juliette's, added, "And to our love!"

CHAPTER VII

THE SECRET OF THE SAFE

THE afternoon of the next day but one, as the three accomplices sat together in the office of the Maharajah's representative, waiting for the hour of Baron Plücke's arrival, the clock on the mantelpiece slowly struck two.

"The time is drawing near!" cried Nam, rising. "Does each of you know exactly what is to be done? Juliette, you will open the door and show the baron in here . . . I will hide myself behind that hanging . . . do you understand? . . . And remember—not the slightest sign of an emotion that would risk everything, not the least hesitation . . . absolute coolness, eh?"

He had not finished the sentence when the bell announced a visitor.

"Here he is!" cried the comte, rushing to the window. No cab had stopped before the door of the house. Faithful to his habits of economy, the baron had come on foot.

"So much the better!" muttered the Hindoo, entering his hiding place. "Now there will be no fear that the driver might have the bad idea of not recognizing in the person who will come out of the house the man who went in!"

But, an instant after, Juliette appeared with an air of great excitement.

"It isn't he!"

"What!" cried the comte. "Then who is disturbing us at this time?"

"It's his secretary—a young man with black spectacles. I showed him into the drawing-room . . . what shall I tell him?"

The comte stifled a furious oath.

"The scheme has missed fire! Did you hear, Nam?"

The Hindoo came out of his hiding-place.

"Don't let us lose our heads," he said calmly. "We will see. We must receive him and try to find out what this means."

Juliette instantly showed the stranger in.

"M. le Comte," he began, "Baron Plücke requests me to bring his regrets that he is unable to call in person."

"Is the baron ill?"

"No, sir. But he is extremely busy to-day, and it is impossible for him to go out."

In spite of his self-control the comte turned pale. He had understood. There is no business that can stand in the way of making four mil-

lions. He made a great effort to retain his coolness.

"And he has asked you to appoint another hour
of meeting?"

"No, sir."

"You are the baron's secretary?"

"One of his secretaries."

"And you doubtless copied the contract which
he was to sign with me?"

"No, sir, but I am acquainted with the matter."

"Will you permit me to ask you a question?
Am I to see in your coming a desire on the part
of the baron not to go on with the transaction?"

The visitor remained silent a few seconds, then
he answered slowly:

"I know nothing of his intentions. But you
are not ignorant, sir, that we may resolve one
day to undertake a speculation—and the next no
longer find it interesting!"

"Not interesting?" cried the comte, in spite of
himself. "A loan guaranteed by jewels worth
fifty millions!"

"I am making merely a supposition, sir."

"And which I place in the lender's own hands!"

The young man motioned toward the safe.

"Are they here?"

"Here, within reach . . ."

The stranger pushed his glasses up on his forehead, gazed at the huge steel box a moment, and then said coldly:

"You are mistaken."

"How mistaken?"

"That safe is empty."

The comte could not repress a gesture of bewilderment.

"Empty?" But, quickly recovering his composure, he continued:

"Let me tell you, sir, that such a statement is an insult to me. I do not believe that Baron Plücke, whom I consider a gentleman, would have sent you to talk to me in this way . . . to insinuate that the gems upon which I am to arrange a loan do not exist, and to accuse me of swindling!"

"Pardon me, sir," replied the young man, removing his glasses and placing them on the desk by his side. "You misunderstand me. I am only saying that they are not, at this moment, in the safe."

"And on what do you base this supposition?"

"Allow me not to answer your question. It is impossible to give you any explanation at this moment. Rest assured, however," he added, "that perhaps I shall soon tell you things which will amaze you still more!"

"Indeed, sir—and who are you?"

"My name is Lucien Delorme."

On leaving the baron's house he had gone downstairs in a mood of great perplexity. Had not his eyes deceived him? Had he really been in the presence of one of the individuals whom he was seeking? It was difficult for him to admit, a priori, that Comte d'Abazoli-Viscosa, the charming society man, to whom every drawing-room stood open, could be a murderer! And yet—yet —he had seen—it was impossible for him to be mistaken—unless there was some extraordinary coincidence that could be compared only with the accident which had made him suddenly encounter the man who had a bullet in his skull!

Then, after having hesitated for a whole day over the means to use in order to obtain certainty, he had telephoned to Baron Plücke that the comte, feeling slightly ill, had requested him to defer his visit until some other day, and had gone bravely to the comte's house.

"Lucien Delorme?" cried the comte, searching his memory for the association recalled by the name.

"The man who occupied the next room to Mrs. Tankery . . ."

The other leaped to his feet.

"Mrs. Tankery?"

"Murdered one night by two men—the taller

99

one had a bullet in his skull . . . and the shorter one in his leg. Shall I go on, sir?"

The comte, in a tone of quiet sarcasm, answered:

"It seems to me that I do remember all that now. Are not you the young man who gave the police such fantastic details about the crime in the Avenue Mozart, and whom the newspapers called a dreamer. You were even arrested, and then released as a madman."

"Certainly," replied Lucien Delorme emphatically. "But those murderers whose description I gave—those murderers who carried a revolver in each pocket—and who still carry them," he added, looking intently at his companion, "one of whom had a ring on the ring finger—the other a watch in his left vest pocket, and who still have them— would you like to have me tell you who they are?"

"I was going to ask, sir!"

Lucien Delorme had put his gray felt hat on the table, his chestnut-colored overcoat and his yellow kid gloves on the armchair, and, standing erect, with folded arms, he said:

"One, sir, is yourself! The other is the man hidden behind that hanging, holding the fatal wire which he used to strangle Mrs. Tankery and Baron Plücke-Strohé."

For an instant the comte stared at Lucien Delorme in bewilderment, seeming to wonder how he could know all this.

"Sir," he said haughtily at last, "I agree with the police and the press that you are a lunatic. You don't know what you are saying—I will not discuss the matter with you. Accuse me, Comte d'Abazoli-Viscosa, of being a criminal?—Come, come, that would make all my acquaintances laugh. But I do not wish to retain the title of swindler which you so gratuitously bestow upon me.—If it is impossible for me to prove that I have murdered no one, I intend, at least, to give you a proof that the gems exist, and that they are in this safe.—I intend to do for you what I have never yet done for anyone in the world: I am going to show them to you!"

He spoke with such assurance that, for an instant, Lucien Delorme felt doubtful.

What if he were mistaken?

But no—there was no error—he had only to look around him—that empty safe—those men who carried in their very bodies an irrefutable description—the revolvers with which they were armed—the steel wire in the hands of the man concealed behind yonder portière, ready to spring out—they were undoubtedly two villains, capable of the worst crimes.

101

With a rapid, cautious movement, he felt for the revolver in his pocket.

Meanwhile the comte had quietly taken a key from one of the drawers in his desk. Then, after going to the safe and carefully turning the knobs several times, he put it in the lock.

The heavy door turned on its hinges.

Lucien Delorme took a step forward and, looking into the deep chest, exclaimed triumphantly:

"There's nothing in it!"

"No," said the comte, in a loud voice, "but don't be troubled, sir, it will not always be empty!"

Then the young man realized the full extent of his imprudence.

Suspecting the individual whom he had seen in Baron Plücke's drawing-room to be the man he sought, he had come to his home to make sure of the fact without thinking of the danger he was running; he had gone with bowed head into a snare he had set for himself.

Now he was at this man's mercy.

He rapidly tried to grasp the revolver in his pocket, determined to sell his life dearly.

There was no time to do so. The Hindoo had leaped from his hiding-place and seized his arms in a vise, completely paralyzing him.

"Scoundrels!" he cried.

"Be kind enough to sit down, sir," sneered the

comte, "so that we can have a little conversation."

Then, after lighting a cigarette, he continued:

"Don't you think, sir, that, after all, life is a queer thing? One day we do not know each other, the next we meet, ready to rush at each other's throats. How much more quietly we should live, however, if we did not have the irresistible mania for troubling ourselves about what does not concern us?—I do not yet understand your motive for meddling with our affairs! Are you a policeman?—No, you are too clumsy for that. Are you the baron's adviser? —Not that either!—You are not even his secretary, though you told me so just now. You see, sir, that I am well informed. Then by what right do you come to prevent me from carrying to a successful end the speculation I had undertaken?—I don't know that you represent public honesty?—So you are acting from a purely personal standpoint!—And why?"

Then, as Lucien Delorme did not answer, he went on:

"In some way, of which I am ignorant, you were informed of certain peculiarities concerning the murderers of Mrs. Tankery. You knew details of the crime so perfectly accurate that it might have been supposed you had witnessed the whole scene, hidden somewhere in the room it-self. What did you do? Instead of prudently keeping silent, you had nothing more pressing than to tell the whole story to the police—first mistake! You were arrested and, let me tell you, that you were in luck to have been released so easily. Innocent men have been condemned for less than that! Second mistake—you lent your assistance, without any necessity, to Baron Plücke, who could not console himself for having, thanks to us, inherited a large fortune, in order to permit him to take up an old affair that everybody had forgotten. Third mistake—finally, you came here, to my residence, to brave me and deliver yourself to my vengeance with a bold-ness that, undoubtedly, proceeds wholly from ig-norance! Have you never thought, sir, that there are secrets whose weight is heavy to carry, and whose revelation may cost those who betray them very dearly?"

"I know," replied Lucien Delorme vehemently, "that you are murderers and, besides, I need, for that discovery, only the steel wire in your hands."

"You have nothing to fear from it," said the comte in a jeering tone. "It is used only for the unfortunates whom it is humane to make suffer as little as possible! A different punishment awaits the indiscreet—Ah! You see that safes do not contain jewels?—Well, sir, you will look more closely still and reflect upon the danger of meddling with what does not concern you—your secret will remain shut up there through all eternity . . ."

Lucien Delorme could no longer doubt the kind of horrible death which awaited him.

"Help!"

But his cries were stifled in his throat. The Hindoo's fingers were pressed upon his mouth like a tight gag.

For an instant the two accomplices listened anxiously, their ears strained to hear any sound. But their victim's despairing call had not been noticed. They could work in all safety.

Vainly the young man, in a final effort, tried to struggle. He could not escape from his assailants, and was quickly subdued.

The tussle was short. Half stifled, he was pushed violently into the open safe. There was no interior division, no compartment that could prevent him from entering. It was a steel coffin, whose sides would not even allow his cries to pass.

The door was closed on him.

The comte turned the knobs, then the key in the lock, and, having replaced it in the drawer of his desk, from which he had taken it a few minutes before, he sat down in his armchair exclaiming:

"Ah!"

"Now," said Nam calmly, taking a seat opposite, "the main thing is to think the matter over; what do you mean to do?"

"I *am* thinking of it," replied the comte. "At any rate, for a ruined business, it is certainly thoroughly ruined!—And yet it was so well planned," he went on in a tone of dull rage. "What was that fool's idea in plunging into the midst of our speculation, like a dog into a game of nine-pins . . . here is the million lost!"

"Perhaps he did not do it intentionally. That's the reason we need not yet despair!"

"What do you mean by that, Nam?"

"Let us reason a little. Remember, has that individual at any time threatened us with the police? Has he told us that his papers were in a safe place, that we should be arrested to-morrow, that he would soon be avenged? Vague phrases: 'you are robbers—you are murderers'— and yet he wasn't always very sure of it!"

"From which you conclude . . . ?"

"That he has acted on his own idea, without having spoken of his intention to anyone, and that we can once more sleep soundly!"

"So, in your opinion, he came here without even speaking of it to the baron?"

"Certainly. The baron, who is less simple, would have prevented him from doing so without taking precautions. There would have been police officers in the neighborhood, and we are the ones who would now be caught. But no, this chap came to your house to make a little personal investigation on his own account, and the turn of your conversation led him farther than he meant to go, the imprudent fellow! Believe me, he's one of those amateur policemen who, becoming informed accidentally of certain items concerning us, has longed to reveal himself, by a master stroke, a great detective, by discovering single-handed the criminals upon whom, until then, the whole force had been unable to seize. The race is not very dangerous, and we have nothing to fear."

He took up Lucien Delorme's hat and looked at the lining, then his overcoat, which he examined at the back of the neck.

"What did I say!" he exclaimed, "tailor in Eu —hatter in Eu—this is a fellow who, landing straight from his province in the Armelin house, had his head turned by Mrs. Tankery's murder."

"And how do you explain the baron's not coming?"

The Hindoo was about to answer when Juliette came in, bringing a telegram.

The comte eagerly opened it, and uttered a cry of astonishment as he read:

> "DEAR SIR,
>
> "I learn from your secretary that you are ill and cannot receive me to-day, as was arranged.
>
> "I hope it is nothing serious and remain entirely at your command.
> > "Yours very sincerely,
> > > "PLÜCKE."

"What did I say?" cried Nam. "That fellow presented himself to the baron as your secretary, just as he passed himself off to you as the baron's. Doesn't this confirm, in the most striking way, all my conjectures?"

Turning toward the safe, he continued:

"He richly deserved what has happened to him. People who want to play the detective must be more cunning than that!"

"Yes," replied the comte, "he's a dreamer. But my poor million has gone all the same. Job deferred is job lost. Will the baron take it up a second time?"

"Don't be so pessimistic. The scheme is too good to be dropped. You must write him a pleasant note, saying that you really are very ill and

your physician orders you to leave Paris immediately—on your return you will resume the negotiations. By that time we will have got rid of
this spoil-sport's body. The thing to be done
now is to explain this young man's disappearance.
He must not be traced here—that might make
mischief . . . give me a pencil and a bit of paper."

And Nam wrote:

> "I am killing myself in despair because
> I cannot accomplish what I have under-
> taken. Notify my family."

"That leaves the field open for any explanation," he said—"and what is his name?"

"Lucien Delorme."

The Hindoo signed Lucien Delorme, then, taking the overcoat, he slipped the folded paper into
the pocket.

"I'll put it and the hat on a slope of the Quai
Javel to-night," he said. "I hope they will be
found by some honest person who will carry them
to the police station. But, for greater safety,
disguised as a peaceful lounger, I will watch near
by to see that they reach their destination. And
now," he added, turning toward the maid, who was
listening in silence, "let us go and pack the trunks,
Juliette—we leave to-morrow for Cabourg."

PART II

TO SEE IS TO FORESEE

CHAPTER VIII

A SENSATIONAL ROBBERY

SEATED in a comfortable rocking-chair on the terrace of his villa, Comte d'Abazoli-Viscosa, the morning after his departure from Paris was watching, between the puffs of his cigarette, the sunbeams reflected in the blue waves of the sea, whose little white teeth were gnawing the sand of the beach.

He was reflecting. Does not fortune most frequently escape us just at the moment we think we have it in our grasp, and is it not the very height of ill-luck to miss a scheme so well prepared just at the very instant success seems ours?

But who was this man who had come to his house in the place of the one whom he was expecting, and what fatality had so suddenly placed this stranger on his track?

Was it not singular that, occupying the next room to Mrs. Tankery in the family boarding-house at Passy, he should have given details of her murder so exact that it seemed impossible he should not have witnessed it?

Was it not incomprehensible that he should know concerning himself, as well as Nam, particulars whose secret both were sure of being the sole possessors, precisely as if he were ignorant of no fact in their past life?

Finally, was it not extraordinary, when the police themselves had not thought of associating the murder of the American lady with that of Baron Plücke-Strohé, he should have divined that their authors were the same and that, as if he had been an accomplice of the ingenious swindle invented by the Hindoo, he should have doubted the existence of the Maharajah's jewels which, until now, had not been done by anyone?

To ask all these questions was not to answer them.

The important point, for the moment, was that, with this man's disappearance, all danger was averted.

His hat and overcoat with the note slipped into its pocket, found on the bank of the Seine, would prevent any other conjecture than that of suicide and, in a few days, someone would draw from the river the body which Nam would throw there after having taken it from its steel prison.

But, before hurling himself so imprudently into the jaws of the wolf from which he was never to come forth alive, had he told Baron

114

Plücke of his conjectures? Had he put him on his guard against his borrower? Had he even merely urged him to be distrustful and cautious?

And, ignorant of what might happen, thinking of the sword of Damocles suspended over his head, the comte, excellent gambler as he might be, did not feel wholly reassured.

Suddenly a voice behind him roused him from his reverie:

"Of what is M. le Comte thinking?"

Turning, he saw Nam looking at him with an ironical expression. As the comte made no reply, he went on calmly:

"Certainly, at this season, it is pleasanter here than in Paris. There's nothing better to cleanse the lungs than this salt air from the sea. But," he added, "you are not of the same opinion? You seem to be a little vexed this morning?"

The comte, with a nervous gesture, flung his cigarette away.

"You see, Nam," he murmured, "I am thinking of the famous saying of a queen of France——"

"Which one? Could it be this: '*Here I am, here I will stay!*' Upon my word, with this brilliant sun and this magnificent sea, she would be decidedly sensible."

"No, you do not know our history—the sentence to which I alluded is: '*Well ripped, my son, the point now is to sew it again!*' "

"Which means?"

"That to have shut this young man up in this steel prison, to have destroyed forever with him the secrets which he ought not to have possessed is very well; but we must now think of the future."

"And then?"

"Doesn't it appear to you full of menace?"

"Why?"

The Hindoo went to pick up the end of the cigarette which was smoking in a corner of the terrace and threw it over the balustrade.

Then, coming back to the comte, he replied:

"Because I do not see very well what we have to fear. Reason upon it a little. Is it our fault if the Maharajah needed money and commissioned us to obtain it? As for this young man, haven't we afforded him the best proofs of our loyalty in showing him the jewels when he came to see us from Baron Plücke, just as we are ready to do it for the latter. If, seized with remorse for having deceived himself so greatly respecting us, seeing his position as secretary endangered by so vexatious an error, he sought refuge in suicide, are we to blame?—No, no, calm yourself, nothing is lost!"

116

"Except the million——"

"Ah . . . !"

The comte lighted another cigarette, and, blowing furiously at the match, muttered between his teeth:

"Oh, yes, you take it very easily—a million, more or less, pshaw! what do you care?"

With the same careful manner the valet picked up the match, which he also tossed over the terrace, then suddenly assuming a familiar tone in strange contrast with the deferential respect he had hitherto shown to the speaker, he added:

"No, my good fellow, I don't turn up my nose at a million—a million is a million to me as much as to you . . . ! Only experience has taught me philosophy—and I remember the precepts of our divine Buddha! So when an affair in which one has risked one's life comes to nothing, the money lost is of small importance . . . I don't understand your way of reasoning, but for myself I don't hesitate. A million can be gained once more, but when your head is cut off, it's done forever."

"Certainly," murmured the comte, "with such reasoning one can go a long way! But that doesn't prevent the spoiling of our plans!"

"And why? We'll see about that on our return. Who tells you that Baron Plücke knows

117

the smallest item of the truth? Why do you make these pessimistic conjectures? Has not a ballad-writer told us that everything in life was arranged?"

An evil light glittered in his eyes and a sinister smile contorted his dark face.

"Do you know what I am thinking about at this moment?—The bitter reflections our poor young man in your safe must be having. He's probably wearing himself out crying for help . . . he pounds, no use . . . he yells! . . . the sides stifle his cries and his sobs die away in the darkness—I heard that at the Ambigu—people have literary tastes, my good fellow!"

He began to laugh ferociously:

"That's where indiscretion leads us! Let us hope he will profit by the lesson. In a week we will go and see. Come," he added, as his companion remained motionless, "rouse yourself a little, hang it! We've lost the fortune, but we must think of material things. The funds are beginning to run low; we must get in some receipts. The noble Comte d'Abazoli-Viscosa can't become insolvent, and it would have a deplorable effect if the tradesmen were not paid."

"That is true," replied the other, rousing himself from his thoughts, "we are here to earn our daily bread . . . Ah! who can say that the

118

sharper's business is a lazy one. Now we must show some of our fellow-countrymen that the Casinos are infested with cheats, and that the only honest games of baccarat are the ones played in our villa. Have you prepared the cards, Nam?"

The Hindoo drew from the pocket of his white apron a dozen packs on which the government guaranty band remained intact and, offering them to him, asked:

"Wouldn't anyone say they came straight from the manufacturer?"

"They are marked in the same way?"

"Yes, in the corners. You can make no mistake in giving them. Luck will favor us again this year. Bah!" he added, laughing, "the excellent cocktails prepared by my care will console those whom ill-fortune persistently pursues!"

"Do you remember, Nam, during our round of the Swiss hotels, that game of poker which lasted four days, and, in the course of which, Juliette, disguised as Princess Volhourski, relieved three young Germans of the nice little sum of two hundred and forty-five thousand francs?"

"A clever trick, they were all madly in love! One would have thought they gave up their money to be agreeable to her. Be more prudent here. Don't have one of those extraordinary runs of

119

good fortune that open the most innocent eyes! When the haul is not important don't be afraid to lose it, though not without adroitly calling attention to the fact. The fine pigeon to be plucked will appear some day, just when we least expect it! Now I'll have the terrace decorated with flowers, and a handsome awning stretched over it. To attract people, the frame must be pretty."

Then, returning to his obsequious tone, he added:

"Shall I bring up your hot water for shaving?"

"Yes," replied the other, also resuming the suitable distance between them. "And then, Nam, put out a white flannel suit, with mauve socks, and a tie and silk handkerchief to match."

"Very well, sir."

The Hindoo retired, while the comte, resting his elbows on the balustrade and looking at the sea, murmured in a weary tone:

"Work!—Always work!—When will it end?"

Two raps on the door of his room suddenly made him start.

"Come in!"

Nam appeared, carrying a telegram on a silver waiter.

The comte carelessly opened it. But he had scarcely read the contents when he uttered a low oath.

"What is it?" asked the Hindoo anxiously.

The other held out the blue sheet:

"Read it!"

The telegram contained these words:

> COMTE ABAZOLI-VISCOSA,
>   VILLA ATLANTIS, Cabourg.
>   Safe opened during the night by wall-
> cutters. Jewels stolen. No trace of
> criminals. Please return immediately to
> state value of robbery.
>   CLAMART, Chief of Detective Bureau.

"The deuce!" exclaimed the Hindoo, amazed in his turn.

For an instant the two men looked at each other in silence, apparently wondering if they were dreaming.

What did all this mean?

"Well?" the comte asked at last.

"Well," replied Nam, shaking his head, "what do you want me to say to you? I don't understand anything about it—unless we are to suppose it is a disagreeable jest on the baron's part . . ."

"The baron is too serious a man to condescend to such childish nonsense. No—in my opinion, this telegram really does come from the head of the detective bureau . . . our house was entered during the night and our safe has been broken open . . ."

"A burglar-proof safe!"

"Are you ignorant that there are tools strong enough to cut through, without difficulty, the thickest steel plates? Only the criminals have had merely their trouble for their pains; the safe was empty."

"Empty? No—You forget that a man was shut up in it!"

The comte struck his forehead.

"That is true—but then——"

He read over the telegram which he still held in his hand:

"But this is very plain.—*Jewels stolen, state value of robbery.* Nothing about any man in there—so they did not find him?"

"Because he was no longer there!—And, as the door was open, he probably escaped through it!"

"But who opened that door?"

"He!"

The comte threw up his arms. "Come, that's impossible! How could he have done it? He isn't the devil!"

"Evidently. But," the Hindoo calmly continued, "what is the use of making all these conjectures? The simplest thing to do is to telephone to the janitress in the Rue Vézelay for more exact information—then we will consult—wait a minute!"

And he ran to the drawing-room to ask for connection with Paris, while his companion, with his eyes fixed upon the bit of blue paper, pondered for a long time.

But for what purpose should he make conjectures? The most extraordinary afforded no explanation. The truth alone could bring a little clearness into the obscure problem which he was vainly trying to solve.

Just at this moment Nam entered, saying with a bitter laugh:

"I am offered forty-eight—that is, about three hours to wait. Oh, when one is in a hurry, the telephone is an excessively practical method of communication! Well," he added, interrupting himself, "here you are plunged again in gloomy meditations.—What's the matter now?"

"All this seems to me so extraordinary," murmured the comte—"I am wondering if this despatch might not be a trap of the chief of the detective bureau to make us return to Paris and arrest us without a scandal."

"No," replied the Hindoo, "I don't think so. If there was any such intention they wouldn't be so polite, you may be sure. The telegraph would already have been set to work, and the police officers of Cabourg would be ringing at the door of the villa."

But his companion drew himself up to his full height.

"My dear friend, people don't lay hands on the representative of the Maharajah of Pandukurrah so unceremoniously! Think of the diplomatic imbroglio that would be created if, by chance, there should be a mistake! Only he can be questioned—*stolen jewels—state the value of the robbery*—what could be more natural? And when Clamart once has us in his clutches he won't let us go again so easily. Do you want my opinion, Nam?"

"Speak out."

"Let us take advantage of being still at liberty—Havre isn't far off; let us go on board a steamer on the pretext of a little pleasure voyage —prudently put the frontier between us and our enemies—we will watch from a distance to see what will happen, and we shall thus have plenty of time to consider the matter."

Nam shrugged his shoulders.

"Absurd and dangerous! That would be the one way to give birth to suspicions against us which, perhaps, do not yet exist, and to attract attention uselessly to certain points which we have every interest in seeing remain in the shade."

"Well, then?"

"We must hold on to the game. Are we called to Paris? Let us go there. Do they demand the accurate list of the stolen jewels? Let us furnish it. Are we asked our conjectures concerning the authors of the burglary? Let us give them. The more false trails there are, the less easy it will be to discover the real one!"

"Yes," muttered the comte, without being really convinced. "But then everything must happen as you say! And nothing is less certain than that. For it is no use for me to ponder, what I cannot understand is how, after shutting a *man* in a safe, jewels are taken out of it! It's no longer a burglary, it's a sleight of hand trick!"

"We shall see!"

But, at that moment, the sound of a hoarse trumpet rose from the shore, and a panting voice cried:

"Ask—news from Paris—the papers have just come—the last despatches!"

"A minute," said Nam.

He set off on a run and, the next instant, returned with a paper which he handed to the comte.

The latter glanced swiftly over the columns with a practiced eye, and suddenly uttered a low exclamation.

"Here it is!"

And he began to read aloud:

NEW SENSATIONAL EXPLOITS OF
THE WALL-CUTTERS.

"To-night a burglary was committed which, through the boldness with which the criminals operated, the value of the stolen jewels, and, lastly, the personality of the loser, will undoubtedly cause a profound public sensation.

"We will give rapidly the first details telephoned to us by the reporter who was sent immediately to the scene.

"It was about half-past twelve o'clock. The janitor of No. 6, Rue Vézelay . . ."

"No. 4," interrupted Nam, who was listening intently . . .

"No," said the comte, "it really was No. 6. Wait, perhaps there is a reason, I'll go on: The janitor of No. 6, Rue Vézelay, who had gone to the Faubourg Saint-Germain, leaving, as usual, the care of the house to his wife, was returning when, passing the ground-floor, he noticed that the door was open. The fact surprised him, because the tenant, a stranger who had moved in a short time before, was a man of regular habits who never had evening callers. On the other hand, his two servants, who slept in the apartment, always came in before ten o'clock. So it was extraordinary that this door should not be closed. Seized by a sudden presentiment, he hastened into his room to get his revolver. Here another surprise awaited him. His wife, sunk back in a chair, was so sound asleep that, in spite of every effort, he could not rouse her. On the table three glasses and a bottle of champagne, still half full, showed that the unfortunate woman must have been put to sleep with the aid of a narcotic by the criminals with whom she had been drinking.

"Then, taking counsel only with his courage, the janitor, holding his weapon in his hand, entered the ground-floor apartment and, turning on the electric lights, set to work to go through all the rooms. At first nothing seemed unusual, except that the place was deserted. There was no disorder, nothing was disturbed. He called, no one answered.

"But when he reached the last room, that is, the one adjoining the next house, he saw with amazement that a large hole had been cut in the wall.

"He went up to it, and his bewilderment increased when he discovered that the opening led to a huge safe, which had been broken open by means of implements lying abandoned on the floor.

"He instantly remembered that in No. 4, that is, the next house, the ground floor was occupied by Comte d'Abazoli-Viscosa, ex-embassy attaché and, as everybody knew, the representative in Paris of the Maharajah of——"

"Go on," interrupted Nam impatiently, "and get at once to the fact; I know all your titles——"

The comte ran his eye rapidly over a few lines, then he went on aloud:

"Then the janitor understood the whole affair. His tenant, as well as the cook and valet, were nothing but skillful wall-cutters. Knowing that the Maharajah's jewels were shut up in Comte d'Abazoli-Viscosa's safe, he had hired the adjoining ground-floor apartment, then profited by the comte's departure for Cabourg where he owns a villa, to make, according to their usual proceedings, a hole that led directly to the gems.

"But, as all the windows were grated, and the disappearance of the bars might have, perhaps, been noticed, they gave a sleeping potion to the janitress, who had drunk without distrust with the servants whom she knew and who, having accomplished their object, could pull the bell of the box themselves and vanish in the darkness. If they had not forgotten to shut the door of their apartment many days would doubtless have passed before the robbery was discovered . . .

"He instantly ran to the janitor of No. 4 and informed him of the facts. The latter had the keys of his tenant's apartment. Calling a policeman all three entered. The comte's safe is in his private office, standing against the partition wall of the two houses, a fact undoubtedly known by the criminals and on which they had built their plan . . . It seemed intact outwardly, and nothing revealed that the back had been removed and the contents seized by bold hands.

"We will give, in another edition, new details concerning this remarkable robbery which, undoubtedly, amounts to several tens of millions, the exact amount cannot be ascertained until the return of Comte d'Abazoli-Viscosa, who has been informed by the chief of the detective bureau.

"The best detectives in the police force have been despatched in pursuit of the criminals, who must be the tenants of the ground floor of No. 6, Rue Vézelay, whose janitor has given an accurate description of them."

The comte stopped. Large drops of perspiration were trickling down his forehead. Crushing the paper with a nervous gesture, he looked at his companion and, shaking his head, asked:

"Well?"

"Well," answered Nam, rubbing his hands joy-fully; "that's fine! I'll even say very fine! I was beginning, myself, to get tired of those famous jewels—blessed be the burglars who have rid us of them! The Maharajah, of course, will not be pleased—but so much the worse—if he makes too much fuss we'll resign. Whatever may come, it's one burden the less for us to carry. Then we must think of everything; this affair gives a definite and undeniable authenticity to your jewels. They have been stolen, so they exist!"

"And suppose it should be discovered that the safe was empty?"

"Who will tell it? Certainly not the burglars —that is an exploit of which we may be very sure that they will not boast!"

"Even if they are arrested?"

"They will never be arrested, because they have nothing compromising in their hands of which they must some day get rid. Can you see how they must have looked when they found nothing after so much labor!"

"But the man?" cried the comte excitedly— "the man—he isn't mentioned in this article!— Yet he was there. I haven't been dreaming: we shut him in."

"The deuce, yes!" replied the Hindoo. "But why does that person trouble you so much?"

"I shall not be easy so long as I do not know what has become of him. If he is dead, where is his body? If he is at liberty, have we not everything to fear from his disclosures?"

"Don't fret. We shall know sooner or later. Everything in its time . . ."

"May Heaven hear you, Nam! You always have a puzzling optimism—a fatalism of your country—if your head was on the guillotine, you would have the same confidence in your lucky star! For my part, this affair seems so incomprehensible that I give up trying to understand it. I'll follow you blindly."

"And you will do right!—Haven't I guided our ship well until now,—and never to the rocks, eh? Well, I shall continue——"

"Then, what do you decide?"

"I have already told you—to brave the storm —to return to Paris, and place ourselves, without delay, at the service of the head of the Detective Bureau. We shall see—boldness, always boldness! Easy enough to be brave when one has all the trumps in hand—adversity is the time to show pluck! And, to begin, you must do me the favor to recover your coolness and behave like a man who has just been robbed of fifty millions worth of jewels—it's a big sum, deuce take it!"

An hour later the comte's auto, with Nam at the wheel, was speeding over the dusty road from Cabourg to Paris.

CHAPTER IX

IN THE OFFICE OF THE CHIEF OF THE DETECTIVE BUREAU

COMTE D'ABAZOLI-VISCOSA had no sooner sent in his card to M. Clamart than the latter ordered him to be shown into his office.

"Everything you have read in the newspapers is correct, sir," said the chief in reply to his first question; "your safe was robbed last night, and unknown criminals have carried off everything that they found there. As to the details, you yourself have been able——"

"I have not yet been to my apartment," interrupted the comte. "I preferred to come here first. I am just from Cabourg—The Maharajah's jewels stolen!" he continued, in a tone of despair. "What am I to do? It was a sacred trust for which I was responsible."

"We will do our best to arrest the authors of this audacious burglary promptly. Have you a complete list of the jewels?"

"Here it is."

"It will be sent at once to every jeweler and every pawnshop. We have already telegraphed to all the frontiers an exact description of the criminals. They won't be able to cross them. And ever since morning the inspectors have made investigations in the quarters where we think they may have sought shelter. But is there no one whom you yourself suspect?"

"I have wondered in vain.—Oh, M. Clamart, I have committed a serious imprudence, and am well punished for it! This is the first time that, when I went away, I did not put the treasure in my charge into the Bank of France! But my mind was disturbed by a great disappointment."

"What was that?" asked M. Clamart.

"I don't think that it would greatly interest you. Yet I will inform you of all the facts, only requesting you, as the public must be kept in ignorance, not to speak of the matter to anyone. For personal reasons the Maharajah of Pandukur-rah had requested me to obtain a large loan upon his jewels! This was easy, as you may imagine. Baron Plücke, whose name is doubtless known to you . . ."

"Certainly."

"Was to advance the sum. Everything was settled. I had only to deliver the security and send the money to India. But on the very day of the appointment one of his secretaries came to me and said that the baron wished to consider the plan longer. I understood. He desired to withdraw. The business was at an end. I had fixed my departure for the seashore for that very evening, glad to have succeeded in obtaining the loan, whose close I had already telegraphed to the Maharajah. I was so upset that, by an inconceivable forgetfulness, I left my jewels in my safe. The next night it was robbed."

"What you have told me," replied Clamart, who had listened to the story attentively, "is, on the contrary, very interesting. It permits me to discover, at the first glance, that the burglary must have been committed by someone associated with you or the baron, who knew all these circumstances. Can you answer for your employees?"

"As entirely as for myself."

"Then we will question Baron Plücke. I'll telephone to him immediately. We have no time to lose."

Taking down one of the receivers, he called: "Hello! 501-71—urgent—detective service."

While he was speaking his companion was thinking that the decisive game was being played at that moment. By Nam's advice he had faced the situation, and now the baron's deposition would

135

perhaps decide his fate. The moment was a serious one, and he was forced to summon all his coolness in order not to betray his emotion.

Meanwhile the chief had left the telephone.

"The baron is getting into his auto and will be here in five minutes to put himself entirely at our disposal. If you have no objection, M. le Comte, we will continue our investigation. You know that our suspicions rest upon the tenant of the adjoining ground floor and on his servants. The first is a man of average height, with Hungarian whiskers, and a very pronounced English accent. The second is a tall man, corpulent and ruddy, and the other a boy about fifteen years old. You do not remember having seen this trio wandering around you?"

"Really, the description is rather vague: I know so many people! And then," he added, laughing, "in the highest society some mangy sheep always slip in, and it is not easy to unmask them."

"That is true," replied M. Clamart. "I'll question the servants in the two houses soon. Perhaps they will give us some useful information."

At that moment the door opened, and the bailiff appeared, announcing Baron Plücke's arrival.

"Show him in," said the chief of the detective bureau.

The financier had already seen in the morning papers, with natural surprise, the account of the burglary.

But at M. Clamart's first words he started:

"I sent no one to Comte d'Abazoli-Viscosa, sir!"

"Yet he came," replied the other in astonishment, "someone from you told me that you would defer your visit until next week."

"What!" exclaimed the baron. "On the contrary, it was you, my dear sir, who, an hour before our appointment, telephoned to me that you were ill, and would write to me to make another appointment."

"I did not telephone to you: on the contrary, I had packed the jewels and was waiting for you!"

As the two men stared at each other in bewilderment, not understanding what had happened, the chief said:

"Well, here is one fact gained: that individual was an accomplice of the burglars. We will have search made for him immediately. Will you give me his description?" he added, turning toward the comte.

"He had an overcoat, cut in surtout style, as well as I remember, a soft hat—and a pair of large glasses on his nose——"

137

"Large glasses on his nose?" cried the baron. "I know him—but he isn't one of my secretaries, he's a young man whom chance threw in my way, and whom I had intrusted with a very special mission, which had not the slightest connection with the Maharajah's loan. I know nothing more about him, and I had given him no message for Comte d'Abazoli-Viscosa."

"What is his name?" asked M. Clamart.

"Lucien Delorme."

"Delorme?" exclaimed the head of the detective force, trying to collect his memories. "Why, I know that name. It has remained engraved on my memory. Oh! in what connection have I heard it mentioned?"

Suddenly he seized a newspaper lying on his desk, and, glancing hastily over it, said:

"Listen."

He read aloud the following paragraph:

"Yesterday evening the overcoat and hat of a man named Lucien Delorme were found on the Quai de Javel. A note was also discovered asking that his relatives should be informed. The cause of the suicide is still unknown. The river is to be searched for the body."

"Yes," he added, in a tone of satisfaction, "I

138

knew I had heard it! Only is it the same person who has committed suicide? People don't kill themselves when they have just stolen fifty millions!"

Comte d'Abazoli-Viscosa listened with apparent indifference, but he secretly drew a long breath of relief. The young man had told the baron nothing and, from that quarter, at present, there was nothing to fear.

Nam was right, we should look danger in the face and avert it by the force of audacity.

When the police official uttered doubts concerning the possibility that the man who had committed suicide on the Quai de Javel could be the same as the burglar of the Rue Vézelay, he had muttered between his teeth:

"Don't worry about that—the body that will soon be found in the Seine will inform you—this Lucien Delorme knows too much to live much longer!"

"Gentlemen," said the police officer, "I have only to thank you. We shall set to work without delay, and I have no doubt of a good and speedy success!"

"Permit me to beg you to devote all your efforts to it," replied the comte. "I am in an extremely painful situation and I have not even telegraphed the bad news to the Maharajah! But have you any farther need of me? Can I return to the seashore while I am waiting?"

"Why, certainly, sir. If I have anything new you may be sure that I will communicate with you at once. Besides," he added pleasantly, "with your auto it is no distance between Cabourg and Paris!"

In the passage the comte and the baron shook hands cordially.

"I condole with you most sincerely," said the latter, "and I beg you to believe that you have my best wishes for the speedy arrest of your burglars. As for me, when the gems are found, I shall be again at your service for the loan. You have my promise."

Three hours after, having made a hasty visit to the Rue Vézelay where they examined, with curiosity, the exploit of the wall-cutters, the travelers returned to the Villa Atlantis.

Night had closed in.

Juliette turned on the electricity and, at the dining-room table, after the comte had given a detailed account of the interview with M. Clamart, the two men consulted concerning what it would be best to do in future.

"One thing at a time," Nam instantly declared. "The jewels will be restored to us when it is necessary. You can believe that when the newspapers announce that they were brought back for a very large sum of money and the formal promise to reveal no names, our burglars, no matter what inferences they may draw, will not contradict it. As for the Avenue Mozart murder, it will soon be an old story, neither more nor less than the one in the Avenue d'Antin. Come, we can sleep soundly. But," he instantly added, "that is solely on condition that the individual doesn't come again to put a spoke in our wheels. So long as he lives he will be a perpetual menace suspended over our heads. First of all, he must disappear."

"That is my opinion, too," replied the comte coldly; "this man is one too many under the sun. Let us lose no precious time in seeking what we do not know, neither how he escaped, nor why he does not speak. For, after all, his silence—his disappearance—you will confess that his conduct is at least queer. Anyone else, as soon as he got out of the safe, would have gone to tell everything to the police."

"No doubt he has reasons for that! Who tells you that, as Clamart believes, he may not belong to the band that robbed us? But no matter! We must set out at once in pursuit of him and see that if he escaped us once he doesn't do it a second time. I'll start my campaign to-morrow."

"And how?—Looking for him in Paris would be like trying to find a needle in a hay-mow!"

"Didn't his hat and overcoat have the name of the provincial shopkeeper?"

"I don't recollect their names, but I remember the city, it is Eu (Lower Seine)."

"On the Northern line, just before you reach Tréport. Four thousand inhabitants. Ancient church, historic chateau belonging to——"

"I didn't ask you to recite a page of the guidebook. The main thing is that it should be unimportant enough for me to find without difficulty a man named Lucien Delorme. How far is it from here by the auto?"

The comte reflected an instant.

"Two hours, perhaps—or two hours and a half."

"I will be there to-morrow, and I don't give myself a week to finish my investigation. Then . . ."

His gesture, imitating the movement of the famous steel wire around the necks of his victims, finished his thought.

"No," said the comte, striking the table, "that would be a blunder!"

"What do you mean?"

"This. To find this man is right. To rid ourselves of him is necessary. But that is not all.
Doesn't it appear to you indispensable that we
should know how he learned facts concerning us
of which everyone should be ignorant. Above
all, that we should know whether he is the only
person who is informed of them? It seems
to me that we have a special interest in guard-
ing ourselves against possible surprises in the
future!"

The Hindoo reflected an instant.

"I do not share your view. What is the use
of arguing with a man who is in your way? To
suppress him is the quickest and surest method.
Besides, how will you make him speak? What
means will you employ? Offer him money? That
is risking the chance of compromising ourselves
dangerously, and perhaps without result. Nor do
I see you burning the soles of his feet, or inflict-
ing the water torture upon him to loosen his
tongue!"

"Nam," replied his companion slowly, "you
have never faced anything in life except its material sides and its lowest realities. Are you then
ignorant of the most powerful and the most irresistible force that there is on earth, the force
which, capable of changing the face of the world,
of making mountains meet, of revolutionizing all

mankind, can alone unseal the lips most firmly closed?"

"And that is——?" asked the Hindoo, in a jeering tone.

"Love, Nam. This man will speak, he will speak when he is in love: we have no secrets from the woman we love."

"And the woman he will love?"

"Will be Juliette."

The latter, who was listening silently, raised her head.

"I?"

"You, my child, who will find yourself, just at the right moment, in his path, and to whose charms he will succumb, like so many others!—What will you be? Dressmaker's model, Russian princess, young widow with dark, light, or red hair? We'll decide about that later. But, whichever it may be, this man, desperately captivated by you, will gradually tell you all that we want to learn from him. And you will not even have the merit of novelty: Delila did the same thing before you!"

"I will do whatever you tell me to do!" replied the young woman.

"It's possible!" murmured Nam, shaking his head rather doubtfully. "But, for all that, I prefer my own way. I would rather have an

144

enemy who no longer speaks than one who risks talking too much. When a transaction lasts a long time one never knows what turn it may take, and the fatal tile drops on your head at the moment you least expect it, while, on the contrary . . ."

At that moment the bell at the gate rang violently.

Both men instinctively grasped their revolvers, ready to defend themselves.

But the Hindoo quickly recovered his coolness.

"Don't let us lose our nerve unnecessarily! Juliette, go down and see who it is."

She returned an instant later.

"Some newspaper men who want to interview M. le Comte."

"Oh!" cried the latter, "I would as lief see policemen. Nam, tell them what you choose."

Two minutes later, in the drawing-room, the Hindoo made the following statements:

"The representative of His Highness, the Maharajah, begs you to excuse him for not being able to receive you. He has gone to bed, ill from the emotions he has just experienced. He does not doubt that the keen-sightedness and skill of the chief of the detective bureau will speedily discover the bold criminals, and that the prince's treasure, which was in his charge, will soon be restored to him. Meanwhile, he would be much pleased if you would thank, in his name, all the persons who, under these sad circumstances, have given him tokens of sympathy, which he deeply appreciates, and assure them that he will do so himself as soon as the state of his health permits."

The reporters having gone, the discussion continued. It was lengthy. At last Nam yielded. Violent and immediate proceedings were deferred. It was decided that they would first try, with the aid of Juliette, to pierce the mystery with which Lucien Delorme seemed to desire to envelop himself. At the first alarm there would always be time to act energetically.

The next morning the comte's limousine, driven by himself, completely disguised by the spectacles and dust coat of a chauffeur, stopped on the road leading from Tréport to Eu.

A man, after glancing around to be sure that no one saw him, got out of it, and walked rapidly away, while the auto went on. The man was dressed in a black suit and wore a white cravat. Small whiskers extended along the sides of his somewhat blotched face, and his broad-brimmed Panama hat showed beneath it a few strands of gray hair. He would have been taken for some business man, more especially one of the private detectives employed by the agencies who conduct discreet investigations for private individuals.

Walking slowly, he reached the first houses of the little city visible about a hundred yards beyond.

Eu is the principal place in the district, quaint and attractive, in one of the most verdant corners of Normandy. A little French history is associated with it. Louis Philippe received the Queen of England there. The Comte de Paris lived there a long time before going into exile. All the archæologists have visited its church, which is several centuries old.

In winter, like a marmot, it sleeps peacefully. But, when summer comes, automobiles and carriages dash through it in all directions. Numberless bathers from the neighboring watering-places trample the grass that has grown between the paving-stones. At this season Nam was sure of passing almost unnoticed.

He soon reached the square in front of the château and, wandering haphazard, turned into a street which rose in a slight ascent and on which he saw shops.

One of the first was a hat store whose front still bore the ancient sign of the corporation, a huge red hat.

He entered resolutely, on the pretext of buying a traveling cap.

Fortune favored him. The proprietor was the most arrant chatterbox who could have been met for twenty leagues around. At his customer's first question he told everything he knew.

"Am I acquainted with Lucien Delorme?—Why, sir, he's one of my customers. I had the honor of supplying his father's hats for twenty years! M. Delorme was a fine man. He used to be a mail collector in Bordeaux and, after his retirement, came to live here in the native city of his wife, who still lives in Eu, Rue de la République. He had a remarkable mind—I've often played manille at the Café des Tribunaux—well, sir, you may believe me or not as you choose, I've never seen him cut himself a single manillon. He sometimes said 'My dear Courboulesque . . .'"

"Yes," interrupted Nam, trying on before the glass an English cap offered by the tradesman, "but his son Lucien?"

"A capital young fellow—I supply his hats, too, as I sell, without boasting, to all the city! He's still very young; it's scarcely more than two years since he came back from his military service——"

"And what does he do?"

"Nothing yet. He's too much of a spoiled child —his father left him a little money, so he's in no hurry to work."

Nam took another cap from the pile the tradesman had brought:

"Hasn't he been in Paris lately?"

"Certainly—they say it's to take care of himself—he went to consult a specialist—I don't know exactly what ails him! For some time his ways have become a little queer. He used to be so lively, went into every pleasure with so much spirit, tennis, horseback riding, going every evening in summer to the Casino at Tréport, and now he scarcely leaves the house. Isn't it a touch of what is called neurasthenia? His mother sent him to a great doctor in Dieppe . . . it seems that didn't suffice, since he has had to go to another one in Paris! Oh, sir, these imaginary invalids!"

"And is he still in Paris," Nam asked indifferently, trying on a third cap.

"He has just come back here—his mother did not expect him. I saw her a few days ago, and she told me that her son would probably remain in the capital, for he was going to be the secretary of a wealthy financier—but that probably didn't work!"

Nam knew enough.

He was taking out his pocketbook to pay the hatter when the latter suddenly exclaimed:

"Look, there he is!"

And the Hindoo saw the comte's visitor, with his huge glasses who, having crossed the street slowly, was turning toward the shop.

It was too late to fly. To hide himself was impossible. He must receive the shock, and let events take their course. What would happen?

But the young man stopped an instant in front of the shop window, looked at the hats, glanced inside, then, having returned the shopman's bow, walked quietly away.

Nam drew a long breath; he had not been recognized.

"For a man who sees bullets in you through your body, he is not especially sharpsighted," he murmured as he left the store.—"It is true that I am very well disguised!—That is really he!" the Hindoo added, watching his victim's figure vanish around a corner. "Ah, he can boast of returning from a long distance! But," he continued thoughtfully, "that providential assistance came to him so exactly at the right moment, that I am now wondering if the criminals did not break through walls and open the safe more to rescue our prisoner than to get possession of jewels which they knew were not there?—In this case, the fellow really would be an accomplice, and that would explain his silence. After all, perhaps the comte and Juliette are right: it is a question which it would be interesting to elucidate."

The truth was much more simple than Nam imagined.

When the door of the steel prison, into which he had been thrown, closed upon him and he heard the steel hinges turn into their bolts, Lucien Delorme believed himself lost.

"Oh, the scoundrels!" he exclaimed—"they are carrying out their threats. The Hindoo is closing the iron shutters of the window—the comte is taking my overcoat—and they will go away, turning the key in the door of the apartment behind them. They have gone perhaps forever! What use would it be for me to call? My cries would not be heard—I cannot escape the horrible death that awaits me."

The thought was more than he could bear: he fell fainting.

How long did he remain unconscious?

He would have been unable to say, when he recovered his senses.

He rummaged his clothing; he had neither matches nor watch. But he discovered that he breathed without difficulty and, therefore, inferred that since the air in his hermetically closed

151

prison was not yet rarefied, only a few hours had passed since he was confined in it.

Suddenly he uttered a loud cry, and fell on his knees to thank God.

He could doubt no longer—someone was coming to his assistance—he was saved.

Men were working for his liberation—there were three of them—one very tall,—the third much smaller than his companions—they seemed to be in feverish haste—they were making the stones fairly fly from the walls—they were attacking the sides of the safe.

What tools were they using?—no sound reached his ears—but he saw them, he distinguished their movements—they were advancing rapidly in their work of rescue.

Suddenly the steel plate yielded, falling backward—the safe appeared to open—a blinding light streamed from outside.

Lucien Delorme sprang to his full height, faltering bewildered thanks.

An exclamation of terror instantly answered: "We're in for it! . . . Everyone for himself!"

And, dropping their tools, the three men rushed toward the door as if the devil had just risen before them.

Lucien Delorme looked around him; he found himself alone in an unfamiliar, unfurnished room;

a powerful electric light, suspended by a wire from the ceiling, was burning brilliantly.

Where was he, and what did all this mean?

But this was not the time to seek an answer. The principal thing was to be free. For an instant he thought of taking the same way as his deliverers. But he hesitated; what if some unknown snare awaited him?

Then he ran to the window, opened the fastening and, springing with one leap into the deserted street, fled into the darkness.

The next morning, by the first train, he returned to Eu.

"I've had enough of my character of amateur detective," he said to himself, still trembling at the recollection of what had happened the evening before. "It's a far more dangerous trade than I supposed, and I won't be drawn into it again. To make investigations in the houses of people who shut you up in their safes! Let Baron Plücke henceforth unravel mysteries alone."

It was by reading the story of the exploits of the wall-cutters, a few hours later, that he understood to what miraculous intervention he owed his safety.

But, when he had been in Eu three days, gradually recovering from his terrible emotions, he found himself one morning face to face with the commissary of police who, on seeing him, could not repress a cry of amazement:

"You?" he stammered—"so you're not dead?"

"Why should I be dead? But you see that I am not!"

"Of course!" replied the other—"but, administratively, that is no reason. The letter I have received from Paris is formal. I am to inform Madame Delorme, with the utmost consideration, of the suicide of her son!"

"Of my suicide?"

In a few words the official told the young man of what had been found on the Quai de Javel.

"So, that's the way the comte and his accomplice found to account for my disappearance," murmured Lucien. "But," he continued aloud, "what is to be done now?"

"Why, what always happens in such cases!— Your decease will probably be inscribed upon the records of the municipality—then a decree will be necessary to obtain a rectification—all this is very annoying for you!— Listen," he added, "I'll give you a piece of advice: go to Paris, see the chief of the detective bureau, and explain what has occurred—perhaps there may still be time to attend to the matter!"

"Well, I'll do it," replied young Delorme emphatically, "I'll go to-morrow and I'll take advantage of the opportunity to tell him something that will interest him. Oh, the wretches, they imagine they have done with me so easily. You have just reminded me of my duty! I'll unmask these criminals and deliver them to justice. I allowed myself to be prostrated for an instant, but I have recovered all my courage. I shall know how to avenge myself!"

And leaving his companion, who did not understand the meaning of these words, he went home at once to pack his valise, to the great astonishment of his mother who, after having heard him say the very evening before, that he would not leave Eu again, was troubled by so hasty a departure, fearing he was suddenly worse.

CHAPTER X

A T the whistle of the station master of Eu, the train which was to take Lucien Delorme to Paris began to move, when the door of the compartment in which he sat suddenly opened, and a woman hastily entered.

She wore a large dust cloak of gray cloth, lined with plaid; a long beige veil, falling from her hat in full folds, covered her face, and she carried in her hand a small light leather bag.

After taking out a book, she put the satchel in the net, removed her cloak and placed it by her side, for the morning was warm, and threw back her veil behind her shoulders, revealing her face.

While pretending to be absorbed in his newspaper, Lucien Delorme was looking closely at his companion, and could not help thinking her charming.

Her movements were lithe and graceful; her bearing was reserved and aristocratic; and her waist looked small and trim in her light, tailor-

156

made suit, which was stylish in spite of its simplicity.

As she seemed buried in reading her novel, he could notice at his leisure the harmonious regularity of her features, the luminous beauty of her large blue eyes, the golden hair that seemed like a tangle of sunbeams over her forehead, the delicacy of her hand, whose glove she had removed to be able to turn the pages of her book more easily, and the smallness of her feet in their high laced fawn boots, which her short skirt displayed.

"Who is she?" he wondered. "Not an actress, certainly—a young society girl would not be traveling alone in this way—a young married woman?—no, I see no wedding ring on her finger —A typewriter?—there are charming ones—the profession is so accessible now!—The most probable thing is that she has been spending a few days with relatives or friends and is going back to work—If I dared I would begin to talk with her—it would pass away the three hours of the journey very pleasantly, but how would she take it? She doesn't look easy to approach!"

Juliette, on her part, missed none of his thoughts, divined his intentions and had no doubt concerning the attraction she was exerting on the young man.

157

Having reached Eu the evening before and, according to the comte's instructions, seeking at once to throw herself in his way, she had seen him the very next morning go to the station and have his trunk registered for Paris.

She had no hesitation. She must take advantage of the opportunity to strike up an acquaintance with him. And she had arranged her plan perfectly since, at the moment the train was starting, she had succeeded in springing into his compartment and was taking the journey alone with him.

And, if he was wondering how he could enter into conversation with her, she was trying to find some way of bringing it about.

Under these circumstances there must be the desired result at the first opportunity. Chance occasioned it.

Suddenly the car, in passing over a switch, was violently shaken, and the glass window of the door on the young girl's side fell, letting in the wind, which fluttered her veil.

Before she could make a movement to close it Lucien Delorme had already sprung forward.

"Mademoiselle, will you permit me?"

And, after putting the window back in place, he continued, in an embarrassed tone:

158

"Or Madame—pray excuse me if I am mistaken . . ."

"Mademoiselle," she answered, smiling.

But the young man did not return to his corner and, taking a seat opposite to his companion, exclaimed:

"How can you read with this continual jarring. We are going at least eighty miles an hour —the letters must dance before your eyes!"

"Yes, they do!" she sighed—"but one must be occupied in some way, or the journey would seem too long!"

She half closed her book, and began to look absently at the landscape fleeting along the horizon; but the conversation had progressed too far for Lucien Delorme to drop it so quickly.

"Have you been in Eu, Mademoiselle?" he said after a moment's silence.

"No—I have come from Onival, where I spent a fortnight with an aunt who invited me to make her a visit! But, O dear, vacation days pass so much more quickly than others. Almost before one has had time for a little pleasure, one must think of going back to Paris."

"To put on the yoke of poverty again?"

"Oh, poverty!" she protested gaily—"not exactly—my life is not so hard!"

"What do you do, then?"

159

"Nothing. When I say nothing," she instantly corrected herself, "it's a form of speech, for I have the responsibility of my father's housekeeping—a small household, for we two live alone together—but that does not prevent having my time much occupied!"

"And am I indiscreet in asking your father's business?"

"He is cashier in a large bank."

"And has he no vacations, that he sends you to take yours alone with an aunt?"

The girl had tossed the book upon the seat by her side.

"Yes," she answered, laughing. "But my father is an old lunatic. He refuses to leave Paris, and declares that as soon as he has passed the fortifications he is bored to death. So you can understand that, when he is at liberty, I don't want to leave him. We walk together all day long about the city; there are so many pretty nooks and corners which are unknown to people! We have a great deal of pleasure in that way, I assure you. But are not you a Parisian, too, sir?" she questioned.

"No. I live all the year round in the city of Eu with my mother."

"And of course you are going to Paris now on a pleasure trip?"

160

He hesitated an instant, then said:

"Not entirely. I have an important errand to accomplish. But it is probable that I shall return to Eu immediately after—unless—do we ever know what the future has in store? If I should tell you what has happened to me recently . . ."

"What is it?" she asked, in a tone of curiosity.

"No," he replied, shaking his head sorrowfully, "it would not greatly interest you——"

She was about to urge him, but the train stopped.

The young girl leaned out of the door to see the name of the station: then, with a rapid movement, her companion raised the cover of the novel she had flung down by her side, and read the two words penciled inside.

Georgette Meunier

"I know her name," he murmured joyously.

Juliette, during this time, was thinking: "If only no one gets into our compartment!"

But no one did come in and, two minutes later, the train moved on.

Lucien Delorme had gradually allowed himself to yield entirely to the charm of his pretty companion. Never had he felt so deeply impressed,

161

and his heart was beating so violently that he thought he should faint.

"She is exquisite," he murmured, "and I should be the happiest of men if I could make her share the intense emotion I feel for her. Deuce take the doctors, the police, Mrs. Tankery's murderers, and Comte d'Abazoli-Viscosa's safe! I want to think of nothing but her. I love . . . I worship her!"

The conversation was resumed; and it must be supposed that it seemed very interesting to both, for neither noticed how rapidly time was flitting.

Suddenly, glancing through the window, the young man was astonished to find that they were passing the fortifications.

"Already!" he exclaimed.

Then he added:

"In a few seconds we shall leave the train—separate—and yet I cannot make up my mind to lose you thus forever—Will you permit me to ask a question?—Could I not have the pleasure of seeing you again?"

"Oh, sir," she answered, blushing, "that is rather a serious matter!"

"I am asking the question most respectfully, believe me. I dare not yet request you to present me to your father. Perhaps he might think this

162

acquaintance formed in a railway car somewhat singular but, meanwhile, you will be kind enough to help me obtain this pleasure."

She reflected a moment: "It is not an easy thing. My time is not my own. If I should be away long the neighbors would notice it, and my father would soon be informed. What should I tell him if he questioned me?"

"Just a few seconds," Lucien entreated, "just time to ask how you are."

"Very well, I will consent!" she said at last— "I'll arrange to take a roundabout way between two errands. We shall have time for a minute's talk. Only a minute, no longer! You will promise not to keep me?"

"I promise—the anticipation of that minute will be a week of happiness for me!"

"In a week then, that is, next Saturday, be in the Garden of the Tuileries, on the terrace in front of the orange-house, at five o'clock. I'll be there."

"So will I—and thank you with all my heart— I shall not live until then."

The train, slackening its speed on entering the station, had stopped.

Lucien Delorme helped the young girl from the car and pressed the hand which, with a gracious gesture, she extended to him.

"Good-by, Mademoiselle Georgette."

"I hope to see you again soon, Monsieur Lucien."

And they found it so natural to address each other in this way that they did not wonder an instant about knowing the names without having asked.

On reaching the street Juliette sprang into an auto, and, sure that her companion would not presume to follow her, ordered the chauffeur:

"Western station."

Waving a friendly farewell with the tips of her fingers, she said to herself in a tone of satisfaction:

"I have done well. He is firmly caught. Now I'll return to Cabourg, and enjoy in peace a week's well earned rest."

The young man watched the vehicle move away, and when it disappeared at the street corner, he murmured:

"Chance is certainly a mighty master! Yesterday, I was only a sick man, sorrowful and discouraged—to-day I feel as if wings had grown and that I am entering on a new life. O eternal miracle of love! I feel capable now of battling against the evil fate which, for some time, has seemed to pursue me relentlessly. In spite of the doctors, I am confident that I shall recover; happiness is the best remedy in the world. And in a week I shall see her again. A week soon passes . . . besides, I shall have plenty to do. I ought not to hesitate merely because I stumble at the first step. I will follow those criminals and deliver them up to justice—if necessary, it shall be a pitiless struggle. I'll go this very afternoon to the chief of the Detective Bureau."

He took a few steps and emphasizing his thought with a resolute gesture, cried:

"I'll have those two hundred thousand francs —they shall be Georgette's dowry, if she consents to become my wife!"

After lunching in a little restaurant in the suburbs, Lucien Delorme went, as he had said, to the Quai des Orfèvres.

M. Clamart could not repress a start of surprise when the doorkeeper brought the visitor's name.

"Strange coincidence!" he muttered, remembering perfectly the drowned man of the Quai de Javel, concerning whom, a few days before, he had sent instructions.

Lucien entered his office, sat down opposite to him, at his invitation, and began:

"I have come from the chief of police of the city of Eu. You have requested him to notify my family that I had thrown myself into the Seine."

"We followed the course customary in such affairs. Here is the report," he added, rummaging, while speaking, through a file of papers lying by his side: "soft gray felt hat, bearing the name of a hatter in Eu—chestnut-colored overcoat, in surtout style—metal buttons, covered with cloth, one missing on the right side—in one of the back pockets a pair of dogskin gloves, yellow ones, on which the size, $7\frac{3}{4}$, and the price, 2 francs, 95 centimes, were still visible."

"All these articles really are mine," cried the young man, "and I am going to make some very serious disclosures, M. Clamart."

"Speak, sir."

"This overcoat and hat were left by me in the residence of Comte d'Abazoli-Viscosa, 4, Rue Vézelay."

"Comte d'Abazoli-Viscosa?"

"Who put them on the Quai de Javel to account for my disappearance, and prevent people from searching for me anywhere except in the river, where he was very certain I should not be found! For, M. Clamart," he went on vehemently, "this scoundrel, aided by his Hindoo servant, had shut me in his safe to starve me to death."

"In his safe?"

"To rid himself in this way of a man who was

too sharp-sighted, and had discovered all his crimes!"

"But, pardon me," said the official, "I know Comte d'Abazoli-Viscosa, and up to the present time, allow me to tell you, nothing would warrant . . ."

"M. Clamart, that person is simply a murderer and a swindler—the Maharajah's jewels have never existed except in his imagination! And I'll tell you something more, the murderer of Mrs. Tankery and of Baron Plücke-Strohé is this same man."

"But, sir," cried the chief of the detectives, more and more amazed, "what proof do you offer in support of such an accusation?"

"Proof? Listen just an instant! The proof of his crimes is carried in this man's head in the shape of a bullet left there. With his accomplice proof also exists in the form of another bullet in the leg which their first victim . . ."

But Clamart did not let him finish:

"Aha!" he suddenly exclaimed, looking intently at him, "you are the very same man whom I examined in the Avenue Mozart. I remember your name perfectly now. Lucien Delorme! That's why it seemed familiar to me. I even arrested you?"

"Yes."

"And you were obliged to admit to the examining magistrate that you had mocked the police by furnishing absurd testimony?"

"I told nothing but the truth, M. Clamart, and it isn't my fault, if . . ."

"Come, sir, I have no time to waste in listening to your nonsense. Shut up in a safe?" he added, shrugging his shoulders. "Comte d'Abazoli-Viscosa shut you up in his safe in the place of jewels that had no existence?"

"Yes."

"I ought to charge you with insulting the magistracy by placing your clothing on an embankment of the Seine to simulate suicide. But I pity you; you don't appear to be in full possession of your senses . . ."

He had pressed his finger on the button of his bell.

A police officer appeared at the office door.

"Show this gentleman out."

And, addressing himself once more to his visitor, who stood staring at him with dilated eyes, no longer venturing to open his lips:

"And don't let me see you ever again, my young friend, with your silly stories, or I'll send you to jail in good earnest!"

Lucien Delorme, utterly astounded, found himself in the street.

"Well," he muttered, "that's pretty strong!"
Then shrugging his shoulders, he continued philosophically:

"After all, so much the worse! Since that's the
way the chief of detectives takes it, I have nothing
more to say! Let the police unravel the mystery
themselves. They don't wish to believe that
Comte d'Abazoli-Viscosa is a swindler and a murderer? Very well, that's their affair! I've had
enough of it, for my part. Once sent to prison
. . . the second time shut up in a safe, from
which I escaped only through a miracle . . .
the third time I'm threatened with arrest if I tell
the truth! Come, come, let each man stick to his
trade and the devil fly away with the two hundred
thousand francs! Money doesn't make happiness.
Georgette will love me without that."

And, with his heart filled with the memory of
his fair-haired traveling companion, he resolved
not to return to Eu, but to wait, with a lover's
impatience, for the meeting she had appointed on
the following Saturday.

But, until then, where should he live?

He could not even think of the palatial hotel
on the Champs-Elysées; on the other hand, to go
back to Madame Armelin's boarding-house, after
what had happened, seemed impossible.

Then he recollected that one of his fellow citizens, who was studying law in Paris, had told him of a quiet little hotel at the end of the Batignolles. He would go there. Hailing a cab: "Driver," he said, "go to the Rue des Apennins, and stop at the Hôtel des Nouvelles-Hébrides."

CHAPTER XI

THE EVENING AT KRAKOWSKA'S

SEPTEMBER had returned.

The summer had been cold and rainy so, like the swallows, the sojourners at the seashore were hurrying back to their winter quarters, some going to their estates for the hunting season, others merely returning to Paris, where life was gradually reviving, with the opening of the theaters, and the restored animation of the boulevard, which had been deserted for two months.

Comte d'Abazoli-Viscosa had been one of the first to leave Cabourg, and had settled again in his apartment on the Rue Vézelay, refusing all the invitations which he never failed to receive every year to spend the autumn in a corner of France, where game was plentiful, in some pleasant château.

Besides, for him also, the season had not been very profitable; he had barely paid his expenses.

The steady rain had disheartened the most sincere good will. Enthusiasm was wholly lacking. People shut themselves up where it was comfortable, without even finding courage to go to the next villa to spend the evening in playing cards.

Nam vainly reminded the comte that it was absolutely necessary to provide for the winter and to have some money in advance; he seemed utterly uninterested in all these matters.

The thought of the lost million constantly beset him. He could not console himself. To be so near success, and suddenly see his dreams abruptly crumble!

He roused himself from his torpor only to listen to the reports of Juliette, who at each visit to Paris found Lucien Delorme more captivated and in love than ever.

"Oh!" he muttered between his teeth, "how joyfully I will make that man pay for my disappointment!"

He waited for the coming of that hour with feverish impatience.

Unfortunately, the young girl had not yet succeeded in obtaining any information from her lover. Except for the tender words he lavished, his lips seemed sealed.

She vainly tried to draw from him some detail of his life at the time he met her; he quickly turned the conversation as if the subject she desired to approach was especially painful.

"You will end by making me believe that you

have been mixed up in some crime, Lucien," she exclaimed one day.

"That is possible, my dear Georgette," he answered, shaking his head thoughtfully; "but not in the sense you mean."

Then, as if he had said too much, he instantly stopped, and since that time it had been impossible to learn anything more.

"Yet he must speak!" exclaimed the comte furiously.

"Ah!" murmured Nam sarcastically, "if you had listened to me, we should have been rid of this fellow long ago, and he would be reflecting six feet underground upon the inconveniences of meddling with other people's business."

"Take things easy," said Juliette, "if we gain nothing by fair words, we can use force."

"That's the way we ought to have begun!" returned the Hindoo. "Besides, now that we are settled in Paris again, you can see your lover more frequently, and hasten the course of events!"

It was in the midst of this that one morning the comte found in his mail an invitation from Krakowska, the famous singer, to spend the evening at her house.

Statuesquely beautiful, gifted with a splendid voice, an excellent actress, Missia Krakowska was famous in Russia, Austria, and Germany; petted, flattered, received at court in these three countries, her renown lacked only the consecration of Paris before undertaking the profitable tour of America.

She was to make her début, a few weeks later, at the opera, in the Wagnerian repertory which was her triumph; and, being settled for the entire winter in Paris, she had gathered a few friends and journalists to have a house-warming.

During one of his trips to Vienna, the year before, Comte d'Abazoli-Viscosa had been presented to her. The representative of a millionaire rajah is not easily forgotten. She had taken care to send him an invitation.

The singer had not wished to incur heavy household expenses for a stay of whose duration she was uncertain, so she had contented herself with hiring by the month a furnished ground-floor apartment in the Rue Jadin, a little street in the Monceau quarter which, a few years before, had consisted wholly of houses and gardens, occupied by numerous artists, but which, like all the rest of this progressive section, was being constantly invaded by five-story dwellings, though these did not succeed in removing the quiet, the stillness, and the solitude of an unfrequented district.

Krakowska's apartment was not very large, but

the four windows of the drawing-room and the dining-room looked out upon the street.

The actress had required only convenience and comfort; as for the rest, as artist and woman, she had given very easily the elegance which the rooms lacked. In the drawing-room she had hung some of the magnificent portraits which the most famous artists had painted of her; flowers, springing everywhere as if in a hothouse, masked the poverty of the furniture in a place where the grace and charm of the mistress of the house admirably replaced curios and valuable ornaments.

The guests were not numerous this evening. She had expected about fifty persons. But the life of Paris has a thousand various demands; scarcely half the number had arrived.

Quality, according to a common expression, made up for the quantity. Besides Comte d'Abazoli-Viscosa, there was Foggarol, the influential musical critic of the hour; Baroness de Vallègre, a personal friend of Krakowska; Rose Planchet, the beautiful artist of the opera; the military attaché of Hungary, Captain Zchklacht; the Marquis de la Torre, President of the Pierrot Club, arbiter of Parisian ultra-fashionable life; twenty more people including well-known clubmen, and charming society women, and finally, Lady Duf-

175

ferton, a very attractive member of the highest English society who, profiting by a brief trip to Paris, had not wished to miss the great singer's reception.

To hear Krakowska sing was always a treat; it was useless for her to resist, she must show her guests that her voice was still marvelous and worthy of general admiration.

Song succeeded song amid unanimous enthusiasm until, visibly fatigued, she finally asked mercy.

"My friends," she said, "your plaudits touch me deeply . . . but please let me take a little breath! While waiting for supper, tables will be brought in. Those who like bridge can take their places at them, the others will chat in the corners. My dear Comte," she added, turning toward the Maharajah's representative, "will you help me arrange the game?"

The latter bowed, and instantly began the work. Bridge, at that time, was still sufficiently fashionable to have several tables filled at once.

He himself refused to sit down, pleading absolute ignorance of the difficult art of doubling and redoubling.

"Use cards which do not come from Nam's hands," he muttered. "I'm too fond of having

176

luck sure to favor me! Besides, I play too often from necessity to do it for my own pleasure."

So he went to join the little group which had gathered in a corner of the drawing-room around the mistress of the house.

"Dear Madame," said the latter to Lady Dufferton who had taken a seat by her side, "you certainly know Comte d'Abazoli-Viscosa, who represents in France the wealthy Maharajah of Pandukurrah?"

"We have already met several times," replied the other, extending her hand for the comte to kiss as he bowed before her.

And in a gracious tone to which her little English accent lent a piquant charm, she added:

"I heard with deep regret, M. le Comte, of the extraordinary robbery of which you were the victim some time ago, and I beg you to believe that my sincere sympathy has been with you under these trying circumstances. But, tell me, were all the jewels stolen?"

"All, Madame; the burglars made a clean sweep."

"And they represented a fortune, didn't they?" asked Rose Planchet.

"Fifty millions."

Such a sum always produced its effect. The attention of the entire company was concentrated with curiosity upon the comte, while each individual secretly admired the calmness and the philosophy with which he endured this cruel trial.

"Well," cried the Marquis de la Torre, "those miscreants did not waste their time! But, sir, have you no hope that they will be arrested?"

"I am absolutely certain of it!" replied the comte, firmly. "I can even tell you that the chief of the detective service, with whom I had a long conversation this morning, informed me that he had probably discovered the right trail."

"And," asked Lady Dufferton, taking a glass of orangeade from the waiter offered by a servant, "who could these audacious criminals be?"

"Pardon me, Madame, for being unable to give you any information: M. Clamart urged upon me the most absolute silence. All I can state, if it interests you, is that after to-day it would be impossible for the robbers to negotiate a single one of the jewels without an immediate arrest. Under these conditions they have everything to gain by coming to terms with me and simply restoring them. I am ready to pay a large sum and promise to withdraw my complaint at once. Still, they will not have wasted their time, as someone said just now."

"Certainly," Lady Dufferton assented. "And

178

you yourself must be in haste to see this treasure restored to your safe!"

"I should speak falsely if I stated the contrary," replied the comte, shaking his head, "for I am in a very painful situation in regard to His Highness, who sees the absolute confidence he reposed in me so poorly rewarded!"

"Yet what has happened is no fault of yours," cried the singer.

"A little, Madame, for I sinned through lack of foresight."

"Pshaw!" said the English lady, looking directly at the comte, "the rascals would have been capitally hoaxed if they had found the safe empty."

But the latter did not wince. He bowed and answered, smiling:

"I don't doubt it, Madame."

And when Baroness de Vallègre who, until then, had listened silently asked, in her turn, what the Maharajah had said when he heard of the robbery of which he was the victim, he replied:

"His Highness relies entirely on the French police: under such circumstances the Orientals have an admirable fatalism."

"That is true," Lady Dufferton assented. "My husband, who is an officer in the Indian army, has told me extraordinary examples of it."

And, fanning herself carelessly, she added:

"Besides, we shall soon know definitely, for it seems that the Maharajah is coming to Paris."

The comte, who was answering a question from the Marquis de la Torre, turned abruptly:

"Pardon me, Madame, what did you say?"

"That I read in a paper the other day," she repeated, "that the Maharajah of Pandukurrah intended to go to France soon to spend several weeks. But," she added, in surprise, "didn't you know it, M. le Comte, and do you learn it from me?"

The comte gazed intently at the speaker for an instant, as if trying to read her secret thoughts.

Why had she spoken in that way? What was the meaning of this lie? Did she know anything? Had she suspected the truth? The wife of an officer in the Indian army, had her husband informed her that there was no such person as the famous Maharajah?

He suddenly divined in her an adversary, and the allusion which she had made a few seconds before to the burglars' disappointment in the presence of an empty safe seemed directed point-blank against him.

But this was not the moment to try to penetrate this woman's intentions; he must repel the

180

attack, and find a plausible answer to such a question.

So, in the most natural tone, he replied:

"This journey has been decided for a long time, Madame. But the English government has not yet given its consent. Be sure that I shall be the first person informed and that I shall not fail to communicate all the details to the newspapers immediately! Until that time, permit me to tell you that these statements are pure conjectures, which have no solid foundation."

The little group had gradually scattered.

Some went to the bridge tables, others surrounded the mistress of the house, begging her to sing again; some, seeing that it was growing late, had prudently retired. Soon not more than a dozen of the guests were left.

The comte's eyes sought Lady Dufferton.

"It is absolutely necessary," he said to himself, "that I should have an explanation with her."

But she was neither in the dining-room nor the drawing-room.

"If only she hasn't gone yet," he murmured. "I'll offer to take her home in my auto, and, if I find that she knows too much, I'll manage with Nam to deprive her of the wish to chatter inconsiderately."

As the Marquis de la Torre passed at that mo-

181

ment, he stopped him and, lowering his voice, said:

"Just a word, my friend! You know everybody, would it be possible for you to give me any information as to who Lady Dufferton really is? She asserts that she is the wife of an officer in the Indian army—is that true?"

"Upon my word," replied the other, "I can tell you nothing positively. All I know of Lady Dufferton is that one meets her in Paris, Vichy, Trouville, in all the fashionable resorts. It seems she has a castle . . ."

"In Spain?"

"No, in Scotland, where she goes to rest at times. She is charming, and I must say that up to the present moment I have never heard anything unfavorable concerning her. However," he added philosophically, "we must believe blindly what she says of herself. We can't ask all the people we meet for their credentials!"

"Of course," answered the comte.

But he suddenly saw her standing near the mantelpiece in the drawing-room and, having thanked the marquis, he went toward her while, after clapping his hands to obtain silence, the nobleman was saying:

"Ladies and gentlemen, our gracious hostess consents to charm us a few minutes more with her divine voice. Will you be kind enough to sit down?"

He had not time to finish. The windows of the dining-room suddenly opened and in the aperture appeared two masked men with revolvers in their hands and daggers in their belts, who sprang into the room, calling:

"Hold up your hands!"

There was general bewilderment.

The bridge-players rose hurriedly. Some tried to escape through the doors, but they were locked. Others rushed toward the windows to shout for assistance, but the intruders had already shut them, and standing before them with threatening weapons prevented any approach.

"Don't let us resist," cried Lady Dufferton, who had maintained her calmness, "they would kill us!"

Her advice was followed and, in the midst of fear-stricken silence, one of the two men, who seemed to have the figure of a Hercules, said loudly:

"Honorable gentlemen and charming ladies, keep cool; no harm will be done you! You will leave here safe and sound. But first you must empty your pockets on this table and place your jewels in the hands of poor fellows who will be most grateful."

"Scoundrels!" Krakowska could not help exclaiming.

"Oh, Madame," replied the other robber, laughing, "that is a very bad word. Excuse us for having used your residence for this little transaction, but we had no choice. Besides, you may be sure," he added gallantly, "that on the evening of your first appearance at the Opera House we will be in the front row of your admirers, and will applaud your success with all our might!"

Comte d'Abazoli-Viscosa watched this scene with an impassive face. He was secretly admiring the boldness of the criminals. To enter an apartment in this way and reduce to submission fifteen persons without having an alarm given, without even being seen by the coachmen and chauffeurs who were waiting a few steps away, was a fine piece of work! The affair was marvelously well planned. He himself certainly could not have done better!

His first movement had been to seize the revolver in his pocket and resist the assailants, but Lady Dufferton had caught his arm:

"In Heaven's name, Comte, don't defend yourself: the attempt would result in trouble for us all!"

So he quietly awaited the progress of events: a robber who finds himself contending with other robbers is always in an amusing situation.

"Each has his turn in this world!" he murmured resignedly.

Meanwhile one of the masked men ordered:

"Ladies and gentlemen, take your places, if you please, along this wall. You will pass, one by one, in front of this table, placing upon it everything of value which you possess. Don't try to deceive us, we shall search you as you pass. Now I warn you that the first cry, the first movement of resistance, means death!"

"Cowards! . . . thieves!" protested Baroness de Vallègre. "Is there no one here to defend us!"

"Baroness," replied the man who had answered the singer, "you may be sure that if, like you, I had a carriage and pair of horses waiting for me at the door, I should not be obliged to use such means! Come," he added, "begin first and be kind enough to give me the emerald necklace presented to your ancestress by King Louis XVIII."

These persons were evidently well informed.

The baroness was compelled to obey: sighing deeply, she laid on the table the historic necklace, her rings, her bracelets, and her brooches—an actual fortune.

"Now your shoe-buckles, I suppose they are not imitation?"

They were merely paste. But the baroness would rather go barefoot than to confess it. So

185

she took off her little shoes and added them to the other articles.

Lady Dufferton came next. She had nothing but a pearl necklace, as she never took her jewels when traveling. Then followed Rose Planchet, Krakowska,. Marquis de la Torre, the Hungarian captain, and others. Comte d'Abazoli-Viscosa was the last.

Without showing too much indignation he gave up his pocketbook, his pearl shirt studs, and his sleeve buttons.

"And in the back pocket of your trousers, my dear Comte?" asked the other robber.

He took out his revolver.

"Aha!" cried the other, "this is a choice piece! M. le Comte must live in an unfrequented quarter to need so accurate a weapon. And now," he added, "the ring on your little finger, if you please?"

It was a large diamond, mounted as a solitaire, on a circle of platinum.

"Gentlemen," said the comte, obeying, "it is impossible to refuse you anything. But I am especially attached to this ring: it recalls a very dear memory. Instead of selling it to some receiver who will give you a tenth of its value I will keep a hundred and fifty louis at your disposal whenever you are ready to return it to me."

186

"Agreed!" replied the other. "It's plain that you understand life; one can always come to an agreement with an honest man of this sort!"

But the comte took no notice of the sarcasm which the speaker seemed to put into his last words, and the latter instantly added:

"Ladies and gentlemen, you will be at liberty in an instant—merely the time required for us to go as we came! But, above all, no noise—wait until we are fairly gone before you call for help. It would not be kind to cause us annoyance!"

They did as they had said and, having pushed open the shutters, leaped out of the window and vanished in the darkness.

For a moment the opera singer's guests, after being left alone, looked at each other in bewilderment: then, suddenly, the danger having passed, they recovered their composure.

Ten voices cried in the same breath:

"Stop thief!"

The first to rush in pursuit of the criminals was the Hungarian military attaché, repeating:

"Stop thief!"

In a second the whole street was in a tumult. People gathered from all sides. Police officers came on a run.

But the robbers were already far away. Vainly was the whole quarter ransacked. Probably an automobile, stationed a short distance off, had carried them swiftly away.

The victims of this extraordinary robbery had nothing left except the meager consolation of making a formal complaint to the officer in charge of the police station in a neighboring street.

They went there.

On coming out the comte returned home on foot: he lived too near, and the weather was too fine that evening to inflict upon Nam the trouble of coming for him in the middle of the night.

He did not grieve for his pearl shirt studs, nor his gold cuff buttons, which were imitation, nor the ten bank bills in his pocketbook, also cleverly imitated, but he did think sorrowfully of his ring.

It had become a sort of fetich. The diamond was one of those he had found in the possession of Baron Plücke-Strohé; he had taken a fancy to it, though he could not have explained why; so he had kept it and had it mounted in a ring which he had worn constantly ever since.

"I will never part with it," he had promised Juliette, "until our wedding day, then I'll put it on your finger!"

But he felt certain that the robbers would bring it back to him—the offer was too large for them to hesitate! Besides, had they not suspected him

of being a colleague? Did they not know him—
the fraternity of thieves is better informed than
the police—and, while reflecting on all this, he was
trying to remember exactly the last words uttered
by the Hercules, which had attracted his attention.

Suddenly he struck his forehead, exclaiming:
"Aha! That very stout man . . . isn't that
the description of one of my burglars? There
were three of them—the second might very well be
his companion, a person of average size. But the
third? . . . I have it!" he added instantly. "It's
Lady Dufferton, the guide. In the Rue Vézelay
she took the part of the groom: in the Rue Jadin
she locked the doors and opened the windows for
her accomplices! And it is for the purpose of
pointing out profitable enterprises that she goes
into fashionable society, pretending to be the wife
of an officer. That is the reason she directed the
conversation this evening to the Maharajah. No
one could know better than she that his jewels
did not exist—and she made me pay for her disappointment over my empty safe by jeering at
me. Ah! the jade—if only I can find her again!
And to think that, one day, I had the imprudence
to receive her in my home to allow her to obtain
the plan of my apartment. She is very clever
—as well as decidedly pretty—and, certainly, I

would never have suspected, in spite of my shrewdness, that Lady Dufferton belonged to a band of robbers!"

When he returned home, he waked Nam to tell him all that had happened during the evening.

"Ill-gotten gains never bring good luck," replied the Hindoo seriously. "I told you not to keep that diamond! But the most intelligent men have such weaknesses for the vanities of this world! As to your suspicions regarding these three individuals, do me the favor not to speak of them to the police; let them unravel the matter themselves. It is always imprudent to put one's fingers between the tree and the bark; there's only one thing to expect—getting pinched!"

And the Hindoo fell asleep again.

CHAPTER XII

THE SNARE

MEANWHILE, Lucien Delorme and the pretended Georgette Meunier were continuing their pleasant idyl.

Not a week passed during which the two young people did not meet in some quiet spot where, away from the crowd, they could chat lovingly for a few minutes.

Lucien Delorme showed that he was more and more captivated with his companion. He came to their meetings with his hands filled with rare flowers, and his lips with tender protestations, but vainly did he entreat her to lengthen their conversations a little. As soon as six o'clock struck, like Cinderella, Georgette rose abruptly and hurried off.

"I must go for my father!" she cried. "That is the reason I went out. If he did not see me he would certainly have suspicions! What should I say if he questioned me?"

Then he let her go with reluctance, not daring to detain her, watching her elegant, slender figure

191

moving away, and answering, with a beating heart, the farewell she gracefully waved to him, never suspecting that she was wondering if he might follow her, and if she could regain the Rue Véze-lay with entire safety.

"Georgette," he said at last, "this situation cannot go on forever. I am suffering too much. Why do you still refuse to utter the final word which would unite us eternally and for which I wait so impatiently in vain?"

They were sitting on a bench in a secluded avenue of the Champs-Elysées. They heard, not far away, the laughter of the children playing. Sometimes one brushed against them while running after its hoop. But, in the shelter of the clump of flowering shrubs that concealed them, they felt isolated and forgotten.

Georgette, with her eyes cast down, made no reply. She seemed to be counting the grains of sand on the path, as yellow as her hair beneath the sunbeams which illumined it.

"Yes," replied the young man slowly, "I have begged you several times to present me to your father. You always refuse. Are you afraid, Georgette, that he will not give us his consent? Yet I have some little property, and am willing to go to work at once. My family is honorably known in Eu. What objections could he make under these conditions? Or is it because you are not yet sufficiently sure of my love? Yet you know that I love you madly, and that the happiest moment of my life will be when you consent to become my wife!"

An almost invisible flush rose to the young girl's forehead and in a slightly tremulous voice, without raising her eyes, she answered:

"My friend, your words touch me deeply. Do not believe that I am insensible to them. I dare not tell you that I share your feelings, but let me hope that you will understand all I experience, without my being obliged to express it. And yet it is true I do still hesitate!"

He had seized her hand and, clasping it gently in his fingers, asked:

"But why?"

"You will laugh at me!"

"I swear that I will not. Speak, Georgette, speak, in Heaven's name! Tell me all that is in your mind."

"Well, this is it. I do not yet know you fully. Your name, your native province, your love for me, yes, I know these! . . . But is this all? It seems as if there was something mysterious in your life which I do not yet know, and which, though I cannot explain the reason, alarms, torments, disturbs me . . ."

193

"Georgette, what have I concealed from you?"

"Oh, very little, doubtless! But, when you have commenced to tell me of your life, why do you stop abruptly? You set off for Paris. And what have you done here? Why does that remain obscure? Oh, Lucien," she added, as he made a movement of denial, "I am ready to love you dearly, but I cannot give my heart to a man who does not show me sufficient confidence to have no secrets from me, who leaves between us room for a doubt, no matter how vague, how unjustifiable it may be!"

"Georgette," replied the young man, pressing one hand on his heart and raising the other as if to call Heaven to witness his sincerity, "there are really some very serious things in that portion of my life—but do not be alarmed, they have not the least association with my honor. Through no fault of my own I have been the victim of so strange a phenomenon, I have been mingled with events so extraordinary, that sometimes I wonder if I have not been dreaming! I will tell you about them some day, Georgette, as you wish, but do not hasten the hour I have fixed for it—for that hour will not strike until, having been presented to your father, I am your promised husband."

Tears rose to the young girl's eyes.

"How unkind you are!" she murmured sadly. "Do people who really love impose conditions! Oh, my dear Lucien, I did not put so many restrictions upon myself when I met you for the first time. My heart gave itself entirely to you, and it seemed to me that, if you did not return my love, I had nothing more to do except die!"

"Georgette," answered the young man, deeply moved, "must your curiosity make me forget my prudence? No—no—do not insist. I will tell you nothing!"

Suddenly he interrupted himself. "Or, rather, yes," he continued, "I will tell you something. I will prove that I am worthy of you, but you will ask me nothing more, afterward, will you?"

Juliette pressed tenderly against him.

"Go on, my dearest."

"Well, this is it—what I have not told you is that, on my arrival in Paris, chance made me aware of a terrible crime committed in the room next to the one I occupied. Now, no one knows the identity of these murderers except myself . . ."

"But how is that?"

"Don't question me, Georgette. These murderers, one of whom occupies a prominent position in the social world, are also the authors of another equally horrible crime, committed several years ago."

"Have you any proofs of this?"

"Undeniable ones, but," he corrected himself, lowering his voice, "so extraordinary that no one can believe it! I spoke just now of mysterious circumstances, Georgette. Come," he added, suddenly interrupting himself, "I went to the head of the detective service to give them to him; well, he laughed in my face, and treated me like a madman!"

"And then?"

"Then? It's all right. I will act alone. I will unmask these scoundrels and deliver them up to justice. That is a duty no honest man should shun. A terrible struggle, too, and full of dangers! Once already they have had the upper hand, and I really believed it was going to cost me my life. A miracle saved me!"

"A miracle, Lucien?"

"At least, the unexpected arrival of people whose coming could be least anticipated. But that did not discourage me. The aid refused by the police I will seek elsewhere—from the nephew of one of their victims. He will have confidence in me, and will not hesitate to grant his assistance."

"Baron Plücke!" Juliette almost exclaimed.

But she controlled herself and, in a very quiet tone, asked:

"Have you spoken to him?"

The young man gazed at his companion with a long, tender look.

"No, my loved one. I haven't yet had time. I want at present to think only of you; there will be time for serious matters later!"

Juliette had risen; she knew enough for the moment.

"Lucien," she said, "before a week has passed I shall have presented you to my father. I need that time to prepare him gently for my marriage. Oh, my love," she added, "if you only knew how happy all that you have just told me has made me!"

He did not detect the irony hidden in these last words.

"Dear little girl!" he murmured, pressing her rosy fingers to his lips.

"And," she continued, "since you have been so good I will do something to be nice to you. I'll promise to get one free evening before the end of the week, and we will spend it together—as an engaged couple!"

"Ah! Georgette," he cried passionately, "how can I thank you?"

"By loving me deeply!" she answered, with a strange fire in her eyes which he mistook for love. "Come," she continued, snatching her hands from his, "it has struck six, I must run away. I shall be late. I hope to see you soon."

"And forever!"

It will certainly not be doubted that, on her return to the Rue Vézelay, Juliette received the congratulations of her two accomplices.

"Well," exclaimed the comte triumphantly, "wasn't I right? Have we not done well to wait and investigate? Now we know that this individual was acting on his own account and that, once rid of him, we have nothing more to fear. 'Dead dogs don't bite!' our ancestors said. Nam, we shall be of your opinion henceforward; Lucien Delorme must disappear!"

"Yet it would have been so simple in Eu," muttered the Hindoo between his teeth . . . "ill-lighted, deserted streets . . . and then by this time, everything would have been finished long ago, while now nothing is even begun!"

"Come, don't be forever growling, you incorrigible grumbler! Let us instead study the means of operating without leaving any trace. This time it is important that the fellow doesn't escape us. We must find something swift, accurate, and cautious to dispatch him to tell that old American woman the way we sent her into the other world —since he knows it!" he added satirically.

The Hindoo reflected an instant.

198

"Where did you say that he was living now, Juliette?"

"Hôtel des Nouvelles-Hébrides, Rue des Apennins, in the Batignolles, room No. 9. The first one on the second story, at the right of the staircase. I drew all these details from him without seeming to do so. Oh, I forgot, the bed is at the right as you enter—there is a large table in front of the window, the gas is put out at ten o'clock."

"Good . . . good . . ." murmured Nam, impressing all he heard on his memory. "I shall go, one of these days, on a little trip to that hotel. Oh, it's a very simple matter to know places!" he interrupted himself, "for we mustn't repeat the deed of Passy. One isn't favored twice by the same luck! Besides, I think I've found a better plan!"

"And that—?" asked the comte.

The Hindoo turned toward the girl:

"You are sure, Juliette, that he doesn't know who you are?"

"Absolutely sure."

She had, in fact, taken every precaution to secure this object. What was the principal thing to avoid? That the young man should ever know from what place she came, and when she left him, to what place she went. Of course she watched carefully to be sure that he did not follow her.

But might not her watchfulness fail some day? Then, by Nam's advice, she used a very simple system to throw him off the track.

On leaving the Rue Vézelay she entered one of the numerous moving picture theaters that swarm on the boulevard, giving uninterrupted performances. There, in a twinkling, she changed her costume in the darkness; garments skillfully arranged permitted a rapid metamorphosis; a blonde wig, a veil, a double hat did the rest.

So, having entered and gone out with the crowd, she was very certain that, even if he was watching, the young man could not recognize her.

This required more time, but it afforded her and consequently her accomplices absolute security. Lucien Delorme could never discover that his fiancée was Comte d'Abazoli-Viscosa's maid.

"Besides," she continued, "he has never thought of doubting anything I have told him about myself, and as for finding fault, he would not have ventured to do so lest he might compromise me."

"Under these conditions, there is no danger that, in case of alarm, we could be reached through your channel?"

"None whatever."

"That's perfect. But now, something else. Are you not to spend an evening with him this week?"

"I promised him that I would."

"And can you manage easily to have him take you out to dinner?"

"He would be perfectly delighted."

"Then listen carefully, Juliette. I will tell you of a little restaurant whose name you will slip into the conversation, giving him to understand that you would like to go there."

"Saying that I had been there with my father and thought it very nice."

"That's it. On the second story there are private rooms looking out upon the street. This is what will happen. While you are eating quietly, an old flower seller will pass, crying her wares. You will manage so that he will go down to buy you a bouquet."

"I should like to see him refuse me anything!"

"Then, pay attention: during his absence, you will pour into his glass the contents of a little vial which I shall give you."

"But if he should notice it?"

"He'll notice nothing. The liquid has neither taste, odor, nor color. But it is a terrible poison which I brought from India. It does not act immediately. Only, two hours after it has been taken, the victim falls lifeless, without any person's ever knowing why. Still, as a matter of prudence, you will leave him directly after dinner."

"That will not be easy. At any rate, for

greater security, I will manage to have him take off those frightful glasses he wears on his nose., And, as undoubtedly he is horribly near-sighted, even supposing that he will not go down to get me the flowers, I shall be able to do it without having him see me."

The Hindoo looked the girl steadily in the eyes:

"Your hand will not shake?"

"No. Is it difficult to make a man who loves you do what you wish?"

"Besides, all my precautions are taken; the auto will wait for you a short distance away; in case of alarm, you need only jump into it."

"But," asked Juliette, "where will you find an old flower-seller, who . . ."

Nam shrugged his shoulders.

"No one serves us as well as we do ourselves; I shall be the old woman."

"Oh," cried the girl laughing, "I shall be curious to see you in this disguise."

"It will suit me better than that of a Prince Charming," answered the Hindoo gravely. "Don't trouble yourself, I shall know how to play my part. But that is not all," he continued. "This is Monday . . . by the end of the week, the whole business must be over . . . When do you see him again?"

"Wednesday."

"Then you can arrange the dinner for Saturday?"

"Saturday it is.   But," she queried, "isn't Saturday the 14th?"

The comte took a little calendar from his pocket.

"Yes, it is the 14th."

"Well then, nothing is more natural than that my father should be detained at the bank, and I should be at liberty!"

"You are improving, Juliette," said the comte. "You are beginning to see the importance of the smallest details in the largest enterprises."

"I attend your school, my dearest," she answered tenderly.

While Lucien Delorme's fate was thus being decided, the young man was slowly returning to the Hôtel des Nouvelles-Hébrides.

"She is mine!" he was crying out in his heart, wild with joy.

Divine, ineffable words! Words thrilling with all his youth, all his love! Everything around him seemed beautiful—a sunbeam was flooding his heart awaking all the songs of spring!

A thousand plans were rising in his mind. Already he saw Georgette, in a white robe, descending the church steps on his arm—at last she would be wholly his own. The little house in Eu would vanish under its wealth of flowers, and he would lead to it his fair, fresh, blushing bride!

The very next morning, he would write to his mother the real cause of his stay in Paris. The good woman who imagined that he was pursuing some long, complicated treatment! But is not love the most powerful of remedies? Were people ever ill when they were in love? Later, he would go to the surgeon again, ask from his scalpel the cure of his evil dream, the strange nightmare in which he had lived for several months—but now he wanted to live wholly for his fiancée, to forget everything else, to let nothing distract his thoughts from his happiness!

As he crossed the threshold of the hotel, the landlady stopped him. She was a most excellent woman, attentive and devoted to her guests, regarding the younger ones as her children, the older as her friends.

"Don't make any noise in going upstairs, M. Delorme," she said. "That poor M. Boistet is very ill!"

This was a young government employee, who had lived at the Hôtel des Nouvelles-Hébrides for three years, occupying the room opposite to Lucien Delorme's. Wasted by tuberculosis, he was dying upon his sick-bed, alone and deserted.

But he had refused to allow himself to be carried to the hospital.

"What's the use?" he said sadly to the physician who came daily to visit him each morning. "I know very well that I shall never recover. What I needed was the air of my native province and my parents' little farm in the midst of the green fields. Oh! why did I ever come to this Paris, the devourer of men and purveyor of tombs!"

The landlady's words troubled Lucien Delorme. He liked the young man and several times, during his stay in the hotel, he had gone to spend a few minutes with him, and carry him books.

"What does the doctor say?" he asked.

"That it is the end. He is dying. A matter of days . . . two . . . possibly three."

"Poor fellow! Do you need me to help you watch him to-night?"

"No," she replied, "I can do very well; I am not tired. And besides, there is nothing to do—except wait!"

"At any rate, you can depend upon me!"

"Thank you, M. Delorme, I know that you have a kind heart."

And the good woman, after putting out the gas, followed her guest up the stairs, and sat down by the pillow of the dying man.

CHAPTER XIII

THE DEAD WHOM WE KILL

THE Silver Pike is an old restaurant on the Quai des Tournelles.

Though it has gradually lost a large share of its reputation and its customers, it is nevertheless still well known among Parisians who are fond of good living; the cooking is excellent and, a rare thing, the quiet is absolute.

The view from the second story is extremely pretty. One can see a whole corner of old Paris —the Palais de Justice, with its imposing silhouette surmounted by the exquisite spire of the Sainte Chapelle and the massive towers of Nôtre Dame.

Below flows the yellow Seine, furrowed by barges which give extraordinary animation to this little branch cut off by flood-gates.

While walking toward the Silver Pike, a few minutes before seven o'clock that evening, Lucien Delorme was radiant with joy.

Georgette had accepted an invitation to dine

with him; Georgette had also consented that they should have a private room. It was the first time that they would be alone together—really alone—at last, alone!

True, she had warned him that she would be obliged to go away directly after dessert, lest her father should return unexpectedly. But what did that matter! They would have two long hours before them, and in two hours how many things can be said—how many vows of eternal fidelity can be made—the decisive word would at last fall from her lips, which would seal it upon his!

Henceforth nothing could separate them; they would belong to each other forever, and this delicious thought made his heart beat high, and hastened his steps toward the meeting so impatiently anticipated.

Yet one little shadow darkened this radiant picture.

The guest in the Hôtel des Nouvelles-Hébrides had died that very morning. Poor M. Boistet had rendered up his soul, without suffering, like a lamp that goes out for lack of oil.

But why think of that now? In life, does not joy always elbow sorrow, is not love perpetually a neighbor of death?

Eternal, unfathomable, mysterious law of the universe! We must bow before it, without seeking

to investigate it, and not spoil rare moments of
happiness by reflections so sorrowful.

As he pushed open the door of the "Silver Pike"
a waiter came toward him and, at his request,
ushered him into a private room on the second
floor.

"A lady will come in a few minutes to ask for
M. Delorme; bring her here."

"Very well, sir, will you make out your bill of
fare while you are waiting?"

On being left alone, the young man went to the
window, but he did not glance at the card the
waiter had given him, nor did he look at the majes-
tic panorama outspread before him in the gathering twilight, pierced, one by one by the lights in
the shops on the quay, and the windows of the
neighboring houses.

"She is coming!" he murmured, gazing at
Juliette's photograph, which she had consented
one day, not without objection, to have taken by
one of the open-air artists who wander about with
their cameras and, for a few cents, give a chance
customer an instantaneous proof surrounded with
a frame or put in a brass brooch.

At last he uttered a stifled exclamation. She!
It was she!

She advanced rapidly, slender and graceful in
her little costume, elegant in its simplicity, and

when she passed under a gas jet, her fair hair shone like a golden flame in the darkness which had gradually gathered.

An instant later, two light raps on the door announced her arrival, and she entered, asking in a mischievous tone:

"I am not too late?"

"Dear one, dear one," he murmured, opening his arms to her, "the clock of love has no hours."

She was examining with a look of curiosity the little room with its smoky walls and low ceiling, from which issued an electric chandelier, whose light was subdued by pink shades.

"This is the first time I have ever been in a private room," she said. "When I came with my father, we dined below. All this seems so strange, Lucien. Is it really I who am here? And what are you going to think of the imprudent girl who accepted such an invitation?"

But the waiter had appeared and was stolidly awaiting his orders.

Lucien had handed the card to Juliette, who looked in bewilderment at the endless list of dishes.

Then she returned it, saying indifferently:

"Whatever you like, dear."

He ordered rapidly, haphazard. What did he care?

He was with her, and that was enough.

"Champagne?" asked the waiter.

The young man glanced at Juliette and, as she assented, he replied:

"Yes."

Then, the man having gone out, Lucien, clasping the girl tenderly in his arms, pressed a long kiss upon her blushing brow, and continued:

"What do I think of this imprudence and folly? Why, my dear Georgette, that you were perfectly right to commit them. Are you not my promised wife? Will you not be my bride to-morrow? Under these circumstances, I don't see what there is so compromising in accepting the invitation of a man who worships you. But tell me, have you informed your father of your plans?"

"Yes, Lucien, I have begun to prepare him. In a few days, I will confess everything and ask his permission to present you to him. Oh," she added smiling, "he loves me too well not to consent to my happiness!"

Lucien's heart thrilled with joy.

"How happy you make me, my darling!" he cried. "For my part, I have written to my mother; she will not oppose our marriage, either, I am sure. Oh! Georgette, if you knew how I love you!"

"I love you dearly, too, Lucien, but," she continued, remembering what she had told Nam, "I should love you still more, if you would take off those frightful goggles you always wear, you would look so much better without them! What is your idea in putting such pieces of glass on your nose? Are you so near-sighted?"

But Lucien slowly shook his head.

"Georgette," he said, "don't ask what is impossible. I cannot give you any explanation on this subject—only I cannot remove my glasses; my eyes, my poor eyes could not endure it! It would be too horrible for me!"

"I don't understand you. What is there so extraordinary in being near-sighted?"

"I am not near-sighted, Georgette; but a singular accident, by giving me a superhuman faculty . . ."

Stopping abruptly, he passed his hand across his brow with a gesture of pain:

"No," he said, "I will explain all this later, and I will tell you some things that will amaze you!"

"Oh!" cried the girl, stamping her foot angrily, "always these mysteries!"

But Lucien drew her gently toward him:

"Georgette," he murmured, "why do you have this perpetual curiosity, and what cause have you to question me in this way so constantly?"

"Why," she answered coaxingly, "because I

211

love you. Nothing that concerns you is a matter
of indifference to me. And I notice that you
answer what I ask with big words: mystery—
miracle—phenomenon! Are not you a man like
every other man, Lucien?"

"No," he answered in a stifled tone, "I am a
being unlike any other in the world."

Then as if fearing he had already said too
much, he instantly went on:

"Unlike—for no one else can love as I love
you!"

Suddenly, in the silence of the street, a hoarse
voice called:

"Flowers—buy my pretty flowers!"

"Lucien," Juliette instantly exclaimed, "go
down quick, and buy me a bouquet!"

"Don't you prefer to wait until we have left
the restaurant, my dear one? We'll go into a
florist's, and you shall choose the prettiest one
he has!"

But, having risen, she had run to the window
and recognizing Nam, cried:

"Look, Lucien, it's a poor old woman. Go and
buy her stock. Never mind if her flowers are a
little faded. It will bring us luck to be charitable,
and it is so pleasant when we are happy!"

And as she signed to the woman to come nearer,
Lucien obeyed.

But, as he left the private room, the change of air covered his glasses with a light mist.

He was obliged to take them off, and while cleaning them with his handkerchief, he turned mechanically toward the door he had just closed.

"Dear little girl!" he murmured tenderly.

Suddenly a cry of amazement was stifled in his throat . . . large drops of cold perspiration stood on his forehead, his limbs tottered under him and he had to cling to the banister of the staircase to save himself from falling.

He saw Georgette leave the window, go to the table, draw from her waist a little metal vial, and pour its contents into his glass.

But he calmed himself almost instantly. It was impossible! He had mistaken her movement—his eyes had deceived him. In an instant, on his return, he would question her and all would be explained.

But he was so disturbed that he forgot to put his glasses on again as he went down the staircase at whose foot the old flower woman was waiting for him.

And, as his eyes, naturally, were fixed upon her, he suddenly uttered a low exclamation:

"The Hindoo!"

Under the rags with which Nam was covered, through the flowers in the basket he was carrying, he had just seen the bullet, the famous bullet which had remained in the murderer's leg, and which denounced him like the brand on a galley slave.

Now Lucien understood all.

The assassins had not given up reaching him. Not having succeeded in putting him to a horrible death in their safe, they had now tried to poison him and, more terrible than all the rest, it was Georgette to whom the task was assigned, and this Georgette whom he worshiped, this Georgette for whom he would have given his life, was their accomplice!

All this passed through his brain like a flash of lightning. All the details of the foul play appeared to him as clearly as if a veil had been torn away. He felt his head fairly bursting with pain, grief, bewilderment, and terror.

Pushing past the flower woman and springing into the street, he fled along the quay, like a madman, before the astonished eyes of Juliette, who leaned out of the window, vainly trying to understand what was happening.

But she did not lose her coolness and, making a sign to Nam to wait for her, she settled the bill herself, and quietly left the restaurant.

The auto was waiting a few steps away. They entered it.

In the car, sheltered by the curtains, the Hindoo

214

quickly stripped off his disguise, and flowers and basket vanished through the door.

Five minutes later, they had returned to the Rue Vézelay.

"I said so!" cried Nam furiously; "we ought to have profited by the fine opportunity we had in Eu to rid ourselves of this individual! Now, we must run after a person who feels that he is hunted and is suspicious. Heaven knows whether we shall ever catch him!"

"Come," replied the comte calmly, "don't fly into a passion, Nam. The scheme has failed, that's true; the man has escaped us again, don't let us waste time in wondering why or how . . . he has extraordinary intuition, or luck favors him strangely. The point is not to lose our heads, and decide what we are going to do!"

"Yes," answered the other, thoughtfully, "this is not the time for recriminations. The minutes are precious; to-morrow, perhaps, it might be too late!"

"But what is to be done?"

"First consider where this young man would probably go when he left the restaurant."

"To the chief of police," replied the comte coldly.

Nam turned pale, in spite of himself, then instantly recovering his self-control, reflected that

—not supposing Lucien Delorme could recognize him, and on the other hand he was wholly ignorant of the identity of his companion—they had no reason to fear.

"All right!" he cried, laughing, "if it gives him pleasure! But what next?"

Then, as his two accomplices remained silent, questioning him with a look, he added:

"He'll go back to his hotel. The hunted animal always seeks its covert. To-morrow morning he will go out, to-morrow he'll return to Eu, to-morrow he'll lodge a complaint against his assailants; but this evening he will return home from the instinctive need of seclusion and rest."

"That is very possible," said the comte. "And then, what do you expect to do?"

"Go, this very moment, to the Rue des Apennins and ask for a room in the Hôtel des Nouvelles-Hébrides; then, in the middle of the night, when everybody will be asleep, silently enter his chamber, and with a good dagger-stroke between the shoulders suppress forever a person whose life is a perpetual menace over our heads."

While speaking he had gradually raised his voice: "For I've had enough of all your combinations and shufflings. You see where all this leads! No . . . no, this time I shall employ radical methods, and I shall act myself to be sure of succeeding!"

"Then do so, Nam!" said the comte.

An hour later the Hindoo presented himself at the Hôtel des Nouvelles-Hébrides, with a little valise in his hand, wearing a duster and the traveling cap he had bought in Eu.

The landlady herself showed him into the room he was to occupy and, while following her down the passage on the second story, he smiled contentedly. A pair of shoes outside the door of No. 9 showed that Lucien Delorme was there.

Midnight had come. The house was silent. The gas had been put out long before. The waiter was in the office sleeping while expecting the arrival of belated guests.

Nam stood watching behind his door, listening with strained ears for the slightest sound. He was a tiger lurking in ambush, ready to spring.

His dark lantern was lighted, his bunch of keys ready, and he had wrapped a black veil around his head and put on dark gloves so that he could not be seen walking in the shadow.

He had already carefully planned his flight. By the side of his window the post of a gas lantern rose along the wall, as is the case in all the small streets. To put out this light, and then let himself slide down the wall would be to him mere child's play.

He recalled the information furnished by Juliette: the bed at the right on entering the room.

The moment had come. Nam did not tremble. This was not his first crime. His hand was steady, his movements were quick. Holding a dagger between his teeth, he stole noiselessly along the passage.

This was No. 9.

He looked through the keyhole an instant, then pressed his ear to it.

No sound.

It was the time to act.

The Hindoo cautiously turned the handle; under his light push the door opened; it was not even locked.

Was the chamber empty?

No. Its occupant was sleeping quietly in his bed, his head buried in the pillow and turned toward the wall, seeming to offer his back voluntarily to the blows of the assassin.

Nam moved his dark lantern around him, holding his breath. On the night-table lay Lucien Delorme's glasses, on a chair his blue suit neatly folded and his straw hat. Then the murderer went nearer, his arm rose and fell with the speed of a flash of lightning.

218

His victim had uttered no cry, made no movement; the dagger had entered to its hilt between the shoulders.

Blood streamed from the wound, splashing the sheets with a large crimson stain.

Lucien Delorme was really dead.

An instant after Nam took the way he had planned and, certain that no trace had been left behind, vanished in the darkness of the night.

The next morning a dead body was found in room No. 9.

CHAPTER XIV

AN INCOMPREHENSIBLE MURDER

THE next morning, on entering Comte d'Abazoli-Viscosa's room, carrying on a silver waiter the smoking chocolate for the early breakfast, Nam, after having opened the blinds, went up to the bed and said quietly:

"This time it's done, this Lucien Delorme will give us no more trouble!"

Then he quickly told the comte what had happened during the night in the Hôtel des Nouvelles-Hébrides.

"You are sure, at least, that you did not miss him?" asked the latter.

The Hindoo began to laugh.

"I'd stake my life on it. The blade of a dagger between the shoulders! People never get over that!"

"Well!" cried the comte, "I'm not sorry that it is over. A good riddance! Without mentioning the fact that I was beginning to get strangely jealous of that young greenhorn!"

"Jealous?" laughed the other.

"Don't laugh, Nam. I was afraid that Juliette was gradually taking her part too seriously. By dint of acting the farce of love we sometimes end by being caught. This isn't the first time that it has happened!"

The Hindoo shrugged his shoulders and, looking at the comte with his little mocking eyes, said:

"Then what's the need of loving this woman? Nothing in life is more dangerous than sentiment!"

"Nam, you know very well that this is a subject which we are not to discuss," replied the comte. "My sole dream is to marry Juliette as soon as I am able to retire!"

"Very well, I don't urge the point." Then he added sedately:

"Your pajamas are ready by the side of the bed whenever you wish to get up."

The latter, after his valet had left the room, stretched himself lazily:

"If Nam has worked well," he murmured, "I have slept well—no bad dreams, no nightmares. Good heavens! What an easy conscience I have!"

He jumped out of bed, then suddenly started, exclaiming:

"By Jove! I put my left foot on the floor first! That's a sign of bad luck for the whole day. It's foolish to be as superstitious as that," he added, smiling, "but isn't that the way with us all in Italy? Oh, if it could be done over again I would choose another native country!"

Then, going to the window, he added:

"Well, it promises to be a beautiful day—a little ride in the Bois will be the thing—an opportunity to meet one's friends."

He let the curtain, which he had drawn a little aside, fall again, and murmured tenderly:

"Dear Juliette, how I long to be able to repay you for all the affection and devotion you give me!"

But just as he was going to press the button of the bell to call her, someone rapped at the door, and the Hindoo appeared.

"M. Clamart, the chief of the detective bureau," he said, "wishes to see you."

The comte started violently.

"The chief of the detective service? Oh! I knew very well that the day wouldn't pass without bringing me something annoying!"

"Tol-de-rol!" answered Nam calmly . . . "show a little coolness. Why do you have so many of these idle fears? Haven't we a right to pass for honest people sometimes? Hang it, you must get over this police phobia a little, my good fellow. Come, keep cool, take some of the liquor I put in your office. Besides," he added, "I shall be in my usual hiding-place, behind the curtain, and I'll listen to what he says to you, ready for anything. Whatever may happen, don't worry."

An instant later the comte joined the police officer, apologizing for receiving him, on account of the early hour, in such an undress costume."

"It is I, on the contrary, who am intrusive in coming to your house so early," replied the latter, "but I had some urgent news for you."

"And on what subject?"

"The wall-cutters who robbed you. I believe that we have at last a good clew."

"Ah!" said the comte, justly astonished. "What is it?"

"I will not relate our investigations or our inquiries since the day when you were in my office with Baron Plücke. You doubted, didn't you, whether they would have the least success? Then, in despair of finding any motive, I returned to my first idea, that the robbery must have been committed by the aid of someone very closely associated with you, who knew all your habits and was aware of all your acts and movements. Now, who would have been better situated for the part of guide than your servants?"

"My servants?"

"So I established a watch upon them as close as it was cautious. I must tell you at once that we have found nothing suspicious in connection with your butler."

"That would certainly have been extraordinary. Nam is as devoted as a watch-dog, if not to me, at least to the Maharajah who placed him here, and to suppose for an instant . . ."

"But," the official continued, "the case is very different with your maid."

"Juliette?" cried the comte, starting up.

"Yes. We have the most serious reasons for believing that she is associated with a band of criminals."

"Impossible!"

"Yet it is so. By carefully shadowing her we have discovered certain things which opened our eyes to others. Do you know, M. le Comte, what your maid does several times a week, toward nightfall?"

"Really, I never asked her. I am very liberal to my servants. When they have done their work, as I am at home very little, I give them their liberty."

"Well, your maid rushes into a moving picture theater on the boulevard. You will say," he hastened to add, seeing the smile which his listener could not prevent, "that love for this sort of entertainment could have no connection with her guilt? But wait. The most curious thing about it is that after having once entered the place she never comes out of it."

"How is that?" asked the comte, trying to understand.

"I mean that after having followed her from the time she sets foot outside of your apartment, we always lose track of her as soon as she has gone into the building. How does she pass out? We do not know. We have never seen her come out. She disappears. And as the manager has told us that there was no secret door through which she could leave unceremoniously, we don't know what to think. But what is to be inferred from all this, except that your maid has very serious motives for evading any indiscreet shadowing and, if she takes so many precautions, it is to prevent having us reach, through her, accomplices whom she is deeply interested in not betraying."

"Yes," murmured the comte, thoughtfully. "But," he added, seeming unable to believe what he heard, "who could ever have imagined this about Juliette? A girl who possessed my entire confidence! And it is she, you say, M. Clamart, who acts as guide to the wall-cutters?"

"I don't state that yet. These are mere conjectures. But we shall soon know!"

"And how?"

"By arresting her!"

"Arresting her?" repeated the comte, slowly; "but don't you think this proceeding would be rather arbitrary?"

"Yes. But in defending itself, society must not always regard means. If she gives us satisfactory explanations of her conduct we shall be ready to release her with ample apologies."

"And if she refuses them, for after all . . ."

M. Clamart shrugged his shoulders and, smiling with a knowing expression, answered:

"M. le Comte, a woman always ends by speaking! A man often obstinately keeps his secret—prayers, threats, tempting dishes, nothing will unseal his lips. But a woman! I don't recall a single instance, in my long service as a police officer, in which we have not succeeded in loosening a woman's tongue . . . Before a week has passed your Juliette will have told us not only what we want to know, but even what we shall not ask her!"

"And you are certain of this?"

"Absolutely."

"What will you do?"

"That is our secret. But it is infallible! We shall know her entire life, I tell you, even its inmost secrets . . . Ah! it's lucky that there are women! We should never capture criminals without them. It is always they who, voluntarily or not, sell them! Come, I believe we are on a good track! Now," he added, "as it is useless to cause the slightest scandal in your house, you will be kind enough to call this young woman, and I will beg her to accompany me in the auto-taxi which is waiting for me at your door, with one of my inspectors."

"Very well," replied the comte, without the quiver of a muscle in his face.

Rising, he went to the mantelpiece, and pressed the button of the bell.

An instant later Nam entered.

"Is Juliette in?"

"I think so, sir."

"Send her here immediately."

"Yes, M. le Comte."

When he had gone the comte turned to the police official, exclaiming in a tone of utter consternation:

"It is inconceivable! Juliette a thief! Juliette in league with an association of criminals! Juliette going in disguise to a moving picture theater!"

"Oh," replied M. Clamart quietly, "you haven't reached the end of your surprises: the investigation will doubtless have many others in store for us!"

He had scarcely finished speaking when Nam rushed in like a whirlwind. But his features were convulsed, and his eyes looked wild. His hands were shaking, and his violent emotion almost prevented him from speaking.

At last he made an effort to control himself, and stammered:

"M. le Comte—Juliette—murdered . . ."

Both men sprang to their feet at the same moment.

"Where?" asked the detective.

"In the kitchen!"

They both ran after the Hindoo.

The kitchen was at the other end of the apartment, opening upon a little courtyard, with a long passage leading to it.

When the comte and his companion entered, a terrible sight presented itself.

Juliette was lying in the middle of the room, her face toward the floor, and her arms extended in the form of a cross. Between her shoulders protruded the handle of a knife, whose blade disappeared entirely within the wound, and the blood which had gushed out made a red pool which was gradually extending over the tiled floor.

While the comte had thrown himself beside the poor girl, to listen for the beating of her heart, and the police official was rapidly examining the place with a professional eye, Nam explained in a choked voice:

"She wasn't in the linen room—so I looked for her—and coming in here I found her—so . . . then I ran at once to tell you!"

"Go down quickly," M. Clamart ordered, "and tell my inspector, who is waiting in the auto in front of the house, to come up. Then let the janitor shut the house-door and allow no one to go out—though," he added, "the murderer must be a long distance off already!"

Then, turning to the comte, he asked:

"Well?"

"She is dead," murmured the other.

And he let himself drop into a chair, making desperate efforts not to burst into sobs.

Juliette dead—everything was crumbling around him. Juliette killed by a wretch who had no pity for her youth and his love—the sacrifice was beyond his strength, and his safety was too dearly bought at such a price.

And he could say nothing! It was not even possible for him to abandon himself to his grief, from the fear of betraying himself—and he was compelled to look with an indifferent eye at the body of the woman he loved, without being able to press one last kiss upon her brow, whose warmth still lingered!

"Ah!" sighed the police officer, shaking his head, "here is our clew gone; it's always the same thing. When we think ourselves near the goal, everything crumbles in the hands. But what an extraordinary coincidence it is! At the moment I was going to arrest this woman, she is removed. Wouldn't one think that the murderers had divined my intention?"

Then, noticing his companion's agitated face, he continued:

"Come, M. le Comte, don't be so troubled. Nothing is lost, we'll arrest our scoundrels in spite of this!"

"Ah!" replied the other, "I am discouraged! Ill luck has been decidedly too much against me for some time. The jewels in my charge are stolen . . . I go to a reception and fall into an ambush . . . Now my servants are being killed! What more am I to expect?"

PART III

THE MAN WHO SEES THROUGH WALLS

CHAPTER XV

LITTLE LIGHTS IN THE DARKNESS

LEAVING his inspector to finish the investigations with the aid of the Hindoo, M. Clamart took leave of Comte d'Abazoli-Viscosa and returned to his office.

"The comte is right," he murmured while his car was carrying him rapidly through the streets; "there is certainly a band of criminals attacking him. The robbery of the jewels, the Krakowska affair, this morning's murder, seem to me to be undoubtedly the work of the same individuals, for whom I do not doubt the maid was the guide, commissioned by them to watch her employer's acts and movements. But what I don't understand is why they should have killed her. Unless it might have been done to rid themselves of a troublesome witness and, in that case, to have acted at the exact moment when I was going to arrest her, shows that they knew perfectly well my intentions concerning her. But as I spoke to no one about the matter, who could have informed them so accurately? Did they surmise the cause of my early visit when they saw me arrive with my inspector? Then they had an accomplice close to the victim, in the same house, and constantly on the watch."

After having reflected a long time, as he still found no clew, he continued philosophically:

"When we once have a clew, it's unfortunate to lose it so just at the critical moment; we shall be called clumsy again!"

But, just as he was crossing the threshold of his office, the door-keeper appeared behind him.

"The chief of police of Épinettes," he said, "wishes to see M. Clamart to make an urgent communication."

"Show him in!"

And, as the next instant the door opened upon the official, the chief of detectives exclaimed cordially:

"Good-morning, Risdale, what good wind blows you here?"

"M. Clamart," replied the visitor, "I need your insight to unravel a complicated matter which has just occurred in my quarter."

"Speak . . ."

"I was summoned this morning to investigate a murder committed during the night in the Hôtel des Nouvelles-Hébrides, Rue des Apennins. We found a man in bed, his face pressed into his pillow, and a knife between his shoulders. There was no trace of a struggle or breaking in. The waiter told us that the occupant of this room was a certain Lucien Delorme . . ."

M. Clamart, who, while listening, was signing some papers placed on his desk, started up at this name and, looking at the speaker, cried:

"What did you say?"

"Lucien Delorme," the other repeated. "Profession, student. Resides at Eu (Lower Seine) according to the information furnished by the hotel register."

"It is really he!" murmured M. Clamart, between his teeth. "But go on with your story, Risdale."

"After a few brief inquiries, I sent for the legal doctor and was going to withdraw after saying that nothing must be touched, when the landlady of the hotel ran toward me in great agitation. 'I have been robbed of a corpse!'—'A corpse, Madame?'—'Yes, sir. One of my guests, poor M. Boistet died yesterday morning. The undertaker's men have just come, and we cannot find him!'— 'How is that?'—'The bed is empty, and the body has disappeared!' I shook my head: such a robbery seemed very extraordinary. While the good woman was lamenting, saying that it was her fault, she ought to have watched all night, a sudden thought entered my mind. I took her to room No. 9, where the crime had been committed.—'Turn that man over!' I ordered. The landlady and the waiter uttered a cry in the same breath: 'Why, that isn't M. Delorme, it's M. Boistet!' So it was a dead man who had been murdered, a dead man placed in the bed of another guest! Yet Lucien Delorme had returned that night. The waiter is absolutely sure of it. Besides, his shoes were in front of his door, his clothes were carefully folded on the chairs, even his glasses were laid on a night table, showing that his flight was not premeditated. But, in that case, what has happened that no trace of him can be found? Why has his neighbor's body been placed in his bed? Why has a dead man been stabbed? What part does this man play in this incomprehensible substitution? Then, despairing of unraveling this mystery, I have come, M. Clamart, to appeal to your keen intuition."

But M. Clamart, with folded arms, silently shook his head:

"Lucien Delorme!—Lucien Delorme again! It surprised me, too, not to find him! That man is a nightmare! Now he is hiding stabbed dead bodies in his bed—Oh, my dear Risdale, I've had enough of this Lucien Delorme—you shall begin with arresting the fellow for me and casting me in the shade—then we'll see what all this farce means!"

"Really," said the newcomer, somewhat amazed, "I ask nothing better, M. Clamart, but I must remind you that I do not know him. It would be necessary for you to give me his description. Then," he added, "since you wish it, I will transmit it officially, asking you to begin the investigations whose charge devolves upon you."

"That's fair," replied M. Clamart, smiling. "Let us not waste time in exchanging useless documents. I shall send my agents on his track without delay. Ah! my dear Risdale," he sighed, "we should have been wise to keep him when we had him, after the murder in the Avenue Mozart— you remember the old American lady who was murdered? But the examining magistrate took it into his head to release him, and even with apologies! That's always so, you know; when the police arrest a suspected person, justice sets him at liberty, through a spirit of contradiction. And, afterward, it is we, of course, who are held responsible because so many murderers escape punishment!"

"That is true!" murmured the chief of police from Épinettes.

"However that may be," M. Clamart continued, "from the first day I had the impression that this

Lucien Delorme was connected with the band which I have since vainly pursued, wondering if it is not to make game of me that he imagines crimes, feigns suicides, and murders corpses! Why, my dear Risdale, a few weeks ago he hunted me up in my office to tell me that Comte d'Abazoli-Viscosa had tried to shut him up in his safe to let him starve to death, and that his Hindoo servant strangled people with a steel wire!"

"He came into your office," asked the other, "and you did not arrest him?"

The chief of the detective service looked at him in astonishment, as if he saw a new horizon suddenly open:

"Upon my word, I didn't think of it!"

"I declare!" exclaimed his fellow-officer.

"What can you expect—I sent him to tell his nonsense elsewhere—I took him for a lunatic, such as we have here every day! Besides, even if I had arrested him, having no positive proof against him, he would have been released again! So, what was the use? But, meanwhile, have you searched his room, Risdale?"

"With the utmost care, M. Clamart. However, we didn't find much! A few letters, some bills that seem to prove he is really Lucien Delorme, a student, resident of Eu, as I told you just now . . ."

"That gives some information. I have rather an idea that this name does not belong to him, and that he must have created a false citizenship by stealing papers."

He passed his hand across his forehead, trying to recall his memories.

"Besides, I have corresponded about him with the chief of police at Eu: I'll have his report looked up, and see what he says of the young man."

"There was also," Risdale continued, "a woman's likeness left in a pocket, one of those photos the open air artists take for ten sous, setting included. I brought them all."

"Leave them on my desk, Risdale, I'll look at them later. Meanwhile, not a word to the press, eh?"

"I have already given a note to the reporters at the police office, merely saying that a man named Lucien Delorme had been found murdered this morning at the Hôtel des Nouvelles-Hébrides, and that the police were investigating the crime."

"Very well—but nothing more. No one must be put on the alert. But, now I think of it," he went on, "this Lucien Delorme was for some time in the employ of Baron Plücke, the financier of the Avenue des Champs-Elysées; perhaps I can obtain from him some interesting information."

239

He had not finished speaking when someone knocked at the door of his office and the attendant appeared on its threshold.

"Baron Plücke would like to speak to M. Clamart."

"That's what would be called just in the nick of time," exclaimed M. Clamart; "show him in."

Then, as the chief of police from Épinettes discreetly rose to leave the room, he added:

"Don't go, Risdale, perhaps I shall need you presently."

Baron Plücke entered.

"I was just going to telephone to you, sir," said M. Clamart, "to request an appointment: accident has favored us. But since I certainly owe your visit to some important communication, I will listen first to what you have to say."

"I have come about an old story, M. Clamart," replied the baron; "my uncle's murder. I will not recall the details; you probably remember them?"

"I followed it closely, and recollect the particulars perfectly."

"Then I will proceed directly to the facts. You know that robbery was the motive of the crime, and that all the victim's jewels were stolen by the miscreants?"

"Yes."

"I have left no stone unturned to discover them. Unfortunately, I vainly promised a large reward, engaged the best private detectives, constantly harassed justice, my efforts were futile. The criminals had left no trace behind to find their track. I had lost my last hope when, a few months ago, a foreign lady was murdered in the Avenue Mozart . . ."

"Mrs. Tankery?"

"Certain details given by a young man who declared that, through some incomprehensible phenomenon of telepathy, he had been a witness of the crime, attracted my attention and I wondered if these two crimes had not been the work of the same authors."

"Indeed?" cried M. Clamart, his attention suddenly doubly on the alert.

"So, the next morning I went to find the young man and offered a very large sum if he would place at my disposal a sort of double vision which he seemed to possess."

"Oh!" protested M. Clamart, "double vision! But go on, please."

"This was the way he entered my service, and if I told you nothing about it the last time I came here with Comte d'Abazoli-Viscosa, it was because I considered it useless under the circumstances."

"Well, sir," answered the official, "it was on the very subject of this Lucien Delorme that I, too, wanted to speak to you. No doubt you can give me some information about him?"

"None at all. Who is he? Where does he come from? What does he do? I am utterly ignorant. After having hesitated a few minutes about accepting this commission, he at last decided to go to work. A few days after, in fact, he came to see me and, without going into further details, said that he thought he had discovered a good clew. So imagine my astonishment when, the next morning, I learned, perhaps from your own lips, that he had committed suicide! All this was very strange!"

"And the more so, sir," cried M. Clamart, "because this man never killed himself. His suicide was a sham!"

Baron Plücke, bewildered by what he had heard, remained silent an instant, then he continued:

"But I did not come to speak to you about Lucien Delorme. Allow me to go on in regular order and tell you the whole story. Since yesterday I have obtained a new fact which will perhaps give the investigation a new direction. While looking over some old family papers which I wanted to arrange, I found something especially interesting, and I now have a clew, though a very slight one, that perhaps will enable us to lay our hands upon my uncle's murderers."

"What is it?"

"Among the diamonds carried away by the criminals there was one marked in a special way which would enable it to be recognized among all the rest. It had been given by my great-grandfather to his promised wife, and by a process of which I am ignorant the diamond cutter had found means to engrave microscopically on the lower facet their two initials, A and F, André and Frédéric, whose interlacing bore testimony to the eternity of their vows of love. So it will suffice to seek for this diamond, and then it will be easy, from purchaser to purchaser, to reach the first seller, that is, one of my uncle's assassins!"

"Yes," murmured the chief of detectives, shaking his head, "only . . ."

"Only?"

"Either this gem, in the course of three years, will have passed through so many hands that it seems to me impossible to follow its track or, supposing that it should have remained in the hands of its first possessor, it may easily happen that the peculiarity you describe would not have been noticed."

"May not fortune at last favor us?"

"Granted, but it would be necessary to send a confidential circular to all the jewelers in Paris, in the provinces, and even in foreign countries, and I do not wish to conceal that this would be very burdensome for the result which I anticipate."

"If that's all, I will bear the entire cost, for since this is my last card, I desire all the more to play it! And," added the baron, "think a little of the personal advantage you would derive from having, at the end of so much time, discovered the author of an old crime which no one longer remembered!"

"Oh, I!" murmured the other, with a manner of profound indifference to all these contingencies.

Yet Baron Plücke, without suspecting it, had just touched the sensitive nerve by showing the detective the great renown so striking a discovery would bestow on his intuition and sagacity.

"Very well!" he said. "To-morrow a notice will be drawn up and sent broadcast. Let us hope that it will prove of some service."

"I have a presentiment that it will. But," he continued, "have you no information to ask of me?"

"You have already given it, sir. I merely wished to learn what you knew of this young man who had been in your employ for some time. What you have told me led to interesting conclusions. Logically, as I had always supposed, this person must belong to the band who murdered Mrs. Tankery. How else could he have known all the details of this crime? And, without suspecting it, you yourself aided his plans, by coming the next morning to offer him the opportunity to pursue the investigation on your behalf. This was an excellent way for him to keep in touch with everything that we were doing without attracting attention, and the possibility of warding off the dangers that might threaten his accomplices. That is why, the other day, he had the incredible audacity to come into my office to accuse of the murder of Mrs. Tankery,—whom?"

Then as, by a sign, Baron Plücke intimated that he was unable to guess, the official added:

"The representative of the Maharajah of Pandukurrah!"

"Oh!" cried the other in a choked tone, "that's rather too strong!"

"Isn't it? But have not you some business association with Comte d'Abazoli-Viscosa?"

"Certainly. And I consider him an honorable man, incapable of the least unscrupulous action. To accuse him of such a crime is inconceivable! And," he continued, "you are certain, M. Clamart, that this young man can know nothing about my poor uncle's murderers?"

"Nothing at all—except what you have told him! He was undoubtedly trying to humbug you —only . . ."

M. Clamart thoughtfully scratched his ear.

"Only I am trying to discover the meaning of his sham suicide on the Quai de Javel? Had he swindled you? Had you threatened to have him arrested? In short, had he not any reason whatever for suddenly disappearing?"

"None. I will also tell you that I should never have had an idea that this reserved, diffident fellow, with his excellent manners and very correct appearance, could be a criminal!"

"Ah! in these days nothing distinguishes murderers from men of the world, we are often deceived ourselves!"

While speaking M. Clamart had taken up the papers which the chief of police of Épinettes had laid on his table and was looking mechanically at the portrait of the woman in its little rough copper frame.

Suddenly he interrupted himself, exclaiming:

"What was I saying?"

Examining the photograph an instant, he pressed the button of the bell.

The doorkeeper appeared.

"Has the inspector who went to the Rue Vézelay with me returned?"

"He is waiting in the anteroom, sir."

"Tell him to come in! Darbois," he continued,
holding out the brooch as the officer entered, "do
you know this person?"

The other examined it carefully, in his turn.

"Why," he cried, "that's Comte d'Abazoli-Viscosa's maid, who was murdered this morning."

"Murdered!" exclaimed Baron Plücke, who was
watching the whole scene with astonishment.

"I felt certain that this girl must be the accomplice of the robbers who had been operating
in the comte's apartment, and to-day, while searching Lucien Delorme's chamber, her photograph
was found. What do you infer from that?"

"That she is his accomplice!"

"So henceforth we have the proof that Lucien
Delorme was mixed up in the sensational robbery
in the Rue Vézelay!"

"But, then," cried the baron, as if a light was
suddenly entering his brain, "I understand the
whole! That is why he asked me so many questions about my negotiations with the comte on
the subject of the purchase of the famous jewels!
And, as I had confidence in him, I artlessly gave
the information! And now I think of something
else: it was he who, knowing that I was going to

the Rue Vézelay, telephoned that very morning that the appointment was deferred, for if I had gone that day and taken away the jewels, the operation planned for the same night would have failed."

"By Jove!" replied Clamart, "the whole story links together admirably. You see the interest that Lucien Delorme had in introducing himself into your house! And you helped him by imagining improbable resemblances between the murder of Mrs. Tankery and your unfortunate uncle's. If there had been the smallest connection, we should have detected it at once! This will teach you, my dear sir," he added, "not to try to walk in our footsteps; amateur detectives, believe me, are good only in novels! But reality is very different: each man should stick to his trade."

"If only I had known!" murmured the bewildered baron.

CHAPTER XVI

THE ENGRAVED DIAMOND

A WEEK before all these events a young
man, dressed in fashionable style, with a
small valise in his hand, left the express train
from Boulogne, which arrives at the Gare du Nord
a little before ten o'clock in the evening, and
made his way through the crowd pressing behind the bars waiting for the travelers coming
from England.

It was Anatole, nicknamed Zizi-la-Mouche.

When he was in the street he called a taxi, and
entering gave the address:

"2, Avenue Rachel!"

Five minutes after the auto stopped.

The traveler got out of the car and paid the
chauffeur; then, when the man had gone, he, too,
made a half turn, passed around the corner of
the Boulevard de Clichy and, with a rapid step,
went toward a little café of modest appearance,
situated not far off, whose front illumined the
asphalt with a large square of light, and entered.

Several customers were quietly playing a game of billiards but, at his entrance, no one even looked in his direction.

At the end of the room a man was reading the illustrated papers.

Anatole went straight up to him.

"How are you?"

"Did you have a good trip?" asked the other, raising his head.

"Excellent," he replied, sitting down opposite to him. "The sea was calm and there were not many passengers."

"And your stay passed off well?"

"Certainly."

Then he added, smiling:

"Lady Dufferton, who was in London at the same time, has sent postcards to all her friends to tell them that the weather was magnificent and that the season was commencing brilliantly."

But the waiter had hurried toward the newcomer.

"What will you have, sir?"

"Curaçao bitters."

When the man had gone:

"How is Antoine?" asked Zizi.

"Very well."

Lowering his voice, he continued:

"He didn't come on account of our confounded

250

'description given by all the papers, but he's waiting for me near here."

"And, during my absence, there is nothing new?"

"Nothing that I know of. The police are still running after the wall-cutters in the Rue Véze-lay and the robbers of the Rue Jadin."

"That shows they have legs!"

He stopped; the waiter was putting his glass on the table, but when they were again alone, Augustus asked:

"And you are satisfied?"

"Satisfied—how could one ever be with those English robbers? Of the three hundred thousand francs worth of jewels I took over, I have barely got back thirty thousand francs. What sort of work is that? Yet we may consider ourselves lucky. They quote the difficulties they encounter in getting rid of them, the bad state of trade, the risks they run, all sorts of good reasons. What's to be said?"

He shrugged his shoulders and, slowly lighting a cigarette, added:

"True, the historical value of Baroness de Val-lègre's necklace is difficult to appraise . . . the tale of the Louis XVIII gift would have to be told to some American collector—and that might be dangerous for the dealer. Otherwise, the stones must be taken out, and that deprives it of all its value! But, however that may be, you see ten thousand francs apiece for a performance like that doesn't pay."

"Oh, business nowadays!" murmured the other philosophically.

The two men, as may be supposed, were talking about the affair in the Rue Jadin, so brilliantly executed by the "A" band, during the Krakowska reception.

Selling the booty obtained in such a robbery is always difficult in France. But in England the requirements for the sale of jewels are less rigorous, and pawnshops flourish there with entire freedom.

So burglars daily cross the Channel to get rid of their booty, and Anatole had set out for London to deal with receivers whom he knew.

"So," Augustus answered, "you disposed of everything?"

"Everything . . ."

Then he instantly added:

"Except Comte d'Abazoli-Viscosa's ring. I am very much puzzled about that and have been thinking it over during my entire journey. The offer he made, you remember, to buy it of me at a much higher price than I could get for it anywhere else, shows that its value was certainly tempting."

"And then?"

"Then, if the comte was an honest man, I should certainly have accepted so good a proposition. But I suspect him to be a fellow of our sort, and different in ability, since he has succeeded so well. And I hesitate to enter into relations with him and am afraid that, whatever precautions we may take, he'll get the better of us."

"What do you expect him to do against you?" replied Augustus. "We have a hold on him in the knowledge that his safe was empty, and the jewels he pretended to possess did not exist. For, note one thing,—if he did not have a special interest, a very great interest in not letting people suspect that they were not really robbed, the next morning all the papers would have informed us that the gems were in a safe place and that the wall-cutters had had their labor for their pains."

"Unless he might wish to have the idea believed that the Maharajah's treasure was no longer in his hands, in order to discourage future robbers."

He remained silent an instant, and then continued:

"At any rate, prudence, as a proverb says, 'will save us from the detective bureau.' I've

made up my mind. I will not offer the comte
an opportunity to buy back his ring as he requested. I'll take the stone out of its setting,
and go to an honest jeweler in the Boulevard
Barbès whom I know. A diamond is easily sold;
it is almost cash. I shall have no trouble in getting rid of it."

"After all," murmured Augustus, who had listened to his companion in silence, "perhaps you
are right. And now go home, you must need
rest; I will tell Antoine the result of your journey. To-morrow we will settle our accounts.
Good-by."

"Good-by."

The two men shook hands and Anatole returned
home like an honest agent who has performed his
task.

The next week he walked quietly up the Boulevard Barbès.

"The point is," he was thinking, "to put the
matter skillfully to my good man without getting myself caught. If he suspects that I have
come to sell a diamond for the sole purpose of
getting the money for it, he'll take care to offer
me an infinitesimal sum. So I'll begin by feeling
my way and, while making a little purchase, carelessly mention a stone which I mean to have set
as a scarf-pin. Then, during the conversation,

when he has told me its exact value, I will let him understand that I might be willing to part with it, and will offer to sell it to him."

While pursuing this monologue he had reached a little shop where jewels of all kinds, watches of all sizes, clocks, and various articles of gold and silver made an attractive display.

As he crossed the threshold, the jeweler, after pushing his spectacles upon his forehead and laying on the counter a paper he was just reading, came to meet him with outstretched hand.

"Monsieur Anatole!" he cried cordially. "What good wind blows you here, after not seeing you for so long?"

"Because I was very busy, Monsieur Colleman. I was traveling for my business house. But, thank Heaven, I've at last become a Parisian again!"

"And what can I do for you to-day?"

"Just a trifle . . . But," he interrupted himself, pointing to the sheet of paper, "you were busy? Has the poetic tarantula stung you, and were you writing verses?"

"No," replied the jeweler, laughing, "that is only a circular sent out by the police, at which I was glancing!"

There is no criminal who does not prick up his ears at this word.

"Ah!" said Anatole, immediately interested, "and what is it about?"

"Nothing very interesting. It informs us that in a murder committed several years ago, a diamond, bearing a special mark, had been stolen, and asks those of us into whose hands it may have fallen to notify headquarters."

"And," asked Zizi, in a tone of casual curiosity, "what is this mark?"

"Two letters engraved upon the lower facet . . . I have never seen the stone," he added, "but perhaps one of my fellow-tradesmen may have been more fortunate."

But, while the other was speaking, a sudden thought had entered Anatole's mind, and, without going so far as to imagine that, by an extraordinary chance, the stone in his pocketbook was the very one for which the police were seeking and that this, for lack of others, was the reason the comte seemed to value it so highly, it did not seem to him outside of the domain of possibilities that, during Comte d'Abazoli-Viscosa's life, there might have been a murder followed by robbery.

As he remained thoughtful, the jeweler asked: "What can I sell you to-day?"

Then he answered:

"Oh! I want to make a friend a little gift . . .

256

an alarm clock that won't be too expensive. Will you show me one?"

He had gradually approached the counter on which, a few minutes before, the jeweler had laid M. Clamart's circular and, while the latter, with his back turned, was taking a few alarm clocks from his show window to bring him, he adroitly seized and noiselessly slipped it into the pocket of his coat.

"Here's one at six francs fifty, guaranteed for five years. There's nothing better at the price!"

"I rely on you—there, I like that one in red copper. Wrap it for me. I'm going to do an errand, and will stop for it as I come back."

"Very well!"

Zizi left the shop, muttering to himself:

"Six francs fifty? Not if I know it! We'll see each other again for the alarm clock. But," he added, winking, "thank you all the same for the information!"

Two minutes after, in a neighboring street, he took from his pocket the precious paper.

"Ah," he murmured, "here are the additional details I needed—if I had urged the point, the old rogue would have been quite capable of suspecting something—so it's better to get our information for ourselves!"

Then, glancing at the paper he had unfolded,

257

he began to laugh as he read the word standing out in large characters in one corner: *confidential.*

"Don't worry, Detective Service!" he exclaimed in a low tone, "I shall not cry it on the house tops! Come, now," he added: "an A and an F interlaced—good . . . murder in the Avenue d'Antin—yes! . . . Baron Plücke-Strohé . . . at the request of Baron Plücke-Strohé's heir . . . I don't remember that," he interrupted himself, "but I'll speak of it to Augustus . . . that fellow has a wonderful memory."

He quickened his pace, in a hurry to return home.

"I don't know why this diamond keeps running so in my head."

On reaching his room, he rummaged in a drawer and took out a magnifying glass, such as watchmakers put in their eyes to examine the movement of watches.

Then he looked at the stone intently a moment and, suddenly, cried out:

"Well, I declare!"

He had just discovered on the lower facet of Comte d'Abazoli-Viscosa's diamond the two interlaced letters mentioned in the circular.

A thunderbolt, falling at his feet, would not have caused him more amazement.

"I had a suspicion of it," he muttered to himself. "It is he, and he alone who committed the murder in the Avenue d'Antin. I knew that under the exterior of a fashionable society man he was capable of anything," he added, not without secret admiration.

Then he interrupted himself.

"I shall not denounce him to the police, most certainly. Those things are not done among colleagues, only now I have him! I don't know whether, in offering to repurchase his ring, he intended to play me a trick of his own, but he must behave himself and," he added, rubbing his hands gleefully, "behave himself he shall!"

Then, looking at the diamond which in a sunbeam falling on the mantelpiece where he had put it, was glittering with all the hues of a rainbow, he continued:

"Meanwhile, here is an extremely dangerous gem. If it should ever be found in my hands there would be trouble. What am I going to do with it? Trust it to Antoine or Augustus? Equally dangerous combination! Put it in a safe in the Bank of France? To do that one would need to have one . . . besides, there's the risk of having some inquisitive person go to see it. Let us find something better!"

He went to the window and examined it a moment. The little strips of wood separating the panes were worm-eaten and almost all the putty had fallen out.

So he slipped a knife blade under the one at the right and, with a trifling pressure, made it spring out. Then, in an instant, he made with a gimlet a little hole in which he placed the diamond without difficulty and restored the beading to its place, fastening it with a little strong glue.

"I probably couldn't have stuffed a pearl necklace in there," he murmured, laughing. "But it's an excellent hiding-place for a diamond. Never would anyone searching this room have an idea of going to look there, and unless a glazier . . ."

But he had already taken his hat, and was going rapidly downstairs.

He soon reached the Rue des Dames and, passing in front of a plain house, raised his head and looked at the third story.

"There is a pot of flowers on the window-sill," he said in a low tone: "Augustus is at home!"

Without stopping, he whistled shrilly twice through his fingers, after the fashion of Parisian roisterers.

At the corner of the Avenue de Clichy he turned back an instant and glanced at the house before which he had whistled.

The pot of flowers had disappeared.

So his signal had been heard and answered.

Then he went up the Rue Jacquemont, where he whistled in the same way; a pot of flowers on a window sill of an entresol also instantly disappeared.

"He's notified, too," he murmured in a tone of satisfaction, "the 'A' band will be complete!"

Fifteen minutes later Augustus and Anatole met in the little café on the Boulevard Clichy, where they had already been a few days before, on the evening Anatole had landed from England.

Barely a few instants had passed when a third person, who was extremely stout, entered the café which, at this hour, was empty, sat down at a table near them and began to read the illustrated papers intently.

He did not appear to know his neighbors, but he did not lose a word of their conversation, bending his head forward, from time to time, as if in approval.

It was Antoine.

CHAPTER XVII

FACE TO FACE

IT was seven o'clock when, on that day, Comte d'Abazoli-Viscosa returned from his club.

Going to his office, he called Nam.

"Well," asked the latter familiarly, "has the baccarat been more favorable to-day?"

"No. There are times when ill-luck seems to be implacably against you. Whatever card is needed, one gets the opposite; if it's a low card, one gets a high one, if a high one, a low comes; if one has eight in his hands, the banker throws nine. You see, when fortune has not been rendered favorable, it is decidedly stupid to play."

He laid on his desk two gold chains, a pocket-book, and a silver purse.

"Meager spoils!"

Then he said:

"Lay out my dress coat, and my white cravat. I'm going to treat little Montcerf at the cabaret. It seems that this chap has an old aunt in the provinces, a rich woman who lives almost alone in a lonely château, and whose senile mania is to

pile gold coins in her cellars. I should like to
have some additional information, and there's
nothing like a good Burgundy wine to unloose
the tongue."

"Yes," Nam answered in a low tone, "that
might become interesting; I've always told you
that old families were full of resources !"

"For," the comte added, "it is still too soon to
take up the affair of the Maharajah's jewels,
though we are rid of that disturber who . . . you
are very sure, Nam, that you didn't miss him this
time?"

The Hindoo began to laugh:

"I saw the carriage that took him away for
the autopsy; and besides . . ."

He rummaged in his pocket and, taking out a
newspaper, read:

"*News in three Lines:* A man named Lucien
Delorme was found assassinated yesterday morning in the Hôtel des Nouvelles-Hébrides. Inquest."

He went on:

"While waiting until we can state officially that
we have regained possession of the famous treasure, you might perhaps pay a little friendly call
on Baron Plücke and sound his intentions."

Suddenly the telephone bell began to ring furiously.

The comte unhooked one receiver and held out the other to the Hindoo, signing to him to prepare to answer.

"Hello," said a voice, "is this Comte d'Abazoli-Viscosa's residence?"

"Yes, sir."

"Is he at home?"

"I don't know, sir. I will see. Who is speaking, please?"

"My name doesn't matter. Tell him simply that it is about his ring."

A smile brightened the comte's face.

"I knew it," he murmured: "one can always come to an understanding with honest people of that sort!"

And, by a sign, he informed his valet that he would answer himself the stranger who was at the other end of the wire.

"Here is M. le Comte," said Nam.

"Hello!" said the latter in his turn at the end of an instant, "do you wish to speak to me, sir?"

"Yes," replied the voice. "Excuse my not giving my name, but you will readily understand the motive. Do you still wish to get possession of the ring that was stolen from you in the Rue Jadin?"

"Certainly."

"And what price do you expect to pay for it?"

"Whatever I am asked."

"Under those circumstances it will be easy for us to come to an understanding. Where can I meet you?"

"Here, if you wish."

The stranger remained silent a moment; he was doubtless consulting his accomplices.

"I would prefer another place," he replied at last.

"Then name it yourself."

"If you agree, this evening at eleven o'clock, in the Champs-Elysées."

"Yes. And in what exact spot?"

"In the little avenue that turns around the Concert des Ambassadeurs. We can talk quietly there."

"I'll be there."

The comte hung up the receiver and, turning toward the East Indian, asked:

"What do you say to it, Nam?"

"Nothing," replied the other. "You are robbed of a jewel—you buy it back. What can be more natural? For my part, I don't see how one can attach the least value to such trifles, but that is a matter of personal appreciation."

"Yes," murmured the comte thoughtfully, "I do specially value that ring. And I prize it all the more now that poor Juliette is gone. It seems as if, because I was to place it on her finger on our wedding day, it was now a remembrance of her. Oh! Nam," he sighed sorrowfully, "why did you kill the woman I loved?"

"It was absolutely necessary," replied the Hindoo coldly. "If I had not done it I wouldn't give much for our heads at this time! How could I help it, my poor friend? It is a battle for life. When we confront danger we can't indulge in sentimentality at its risk."

Then, as the comte silently shook his head, not denying that he might not be entirely wrong, he asked:

"Did you notice anything in the conversation you have just had?"

"What was it?"

"That this person is singularly simple to ask the victim to be in a certain spot at a fixed time, without having an idea of falling into an ambush."

"Am I in the habit of bringing the police into my little business affairs?"

"He doesn't know that."

"Perhaps so," murmured the comte thoughtfully, trying to recall the precise words that had attracted his attention from the lips of one of the bold criminals. "But, if according to your opinion," he added, "it is simple-minded not to have considered this possibility, you are no less so, I think, for not believing that he has taken all his precautions in case of alarm."

"That is possible . , ." •

"So I shall act in the most loyal manner. I will go to meet him with three thousand francs, which I will give him in exchange for the ring."

"Three thousand francs!" exclaimed Nam, fairly choking.

"Certainly! Only," he added, lowering his voice, "if, afterward, when we have parted, and he is going away, reassured and confident, to join his watching accomplices, he meets some scoundrel who noiselessly plants a knife ₁between his shoulders and quickly transfers the bank bills from his victim's pocket into his own, I shall not consider myself in any way responsible!"

The Hindoo's eyes sparkled.

"Capital!" he cried. "Now I recognize you. At that place the thick bushes allow one to hide very easily. At eleven o'clock the avenues of the Champs-Elysées are deserted . . ."

"You have understood me, Nam," said the comte. And, looking at each other, the two miscreants began to laugh.

"Ill-gotten gains never profit anyone," the gentleman added. "This knave deserves a lesson!

But make haste with my clothes," he continued. "It's bad form to keep a guest waiting."

The clocks had just struck half-past ten, when Comte d'Abazoli-Viscosa came out of the restaurant on the boulevard, where he had magnificently entertained his guest, the young duke of Montcerf.

The night was dark and cool. Large black clouds were scurrying across the sky, shrouding the moon; it was a favorable hour for mysterious meetings.

"Well, I haven't wasted my evening," murmured the comte in a low tone. "I know all I wanted to learn. The Château of Cérangeville, five kilometers from Caen—the gap in the wall of the park—the servants sleeping in the outside buildings—a watch-dog easily poisoned with a ball of meat, the old woman handling her treasure every night. It seems to me an excellent chance."

Passing under a gas jet, he looked at his watch.

"Twenty minutes yet," he said to himself. "I have time to walk."

He soon reached the appointed spot. The Champs-Elysées was deserted.

Lighting a cigarette, he turned into the little avenue named, and paced slowly, three times, up and down its length.

"If he should not come," he muttered.

As he finished speaking an outline appeared in the darkness, and a small man, slender and delicate, suddenly appeared near him, courteously raising his hat.

"Comte d'Abazoli-Viscosa?"

"Yes."

It was useless to delay for the slightest explanation, so the comte instantly asked: "It is you who have my ring, sir?"

"As I had the pleasure of telephoning you this morning," replied Zizi.

"And you have decided to return it to me?"

"For the payment of a certain sum."

"And what is this sum?"

"Ten thousand francs."

The comte started, unable to believe his ears.

"What did you say?"

"Ten thousand francs."

"But that is preposterous! The ring isn't worth more than a hundred louis! Come, we'll even add fifty by way of extra compensation. That will be more than fair payment!"

"Sir," replied Anatole quietly, "you will give me the price I ask."

In spite of his thorough self-control, the comte could not repress a gesture of indignation:

"I warn you that I will not pay an extortionate

price," he exclaimed. "I came here to transact this little operation fairly. But you would really deserve to have me call the police to arrest you!"

The other laughed defiantly:

"You won't do that!"

"And why?"

"Because it would probably cost you more dearly than me!"

The comte drew himself up with his haughtiest manner.

"What do you mean, sir?"

"Listen an instant. A few years ago a wealthy old man, named Baron Plücke-Strohé, lived in the Avenue d'Antin. One day he was murdered for the sake of robbery . . ."

"I don't see what connection this story . . ."

"Wait a little. The murderer sold all his victim's jewels except a single gem—a diamond. Why? Because this was marked in a peculiar way by which it would have been immediately recognized."

He stopped a moment and then, more slowly, continued:

"M. le Comte d'Abazoli-Viscosa, the murderer, is the man in whose hands it was found. That is why it was impossible for him to part with it, that is the reason he values it so highly! Do you understand? Now," he added calmly, "call the police if you choose, I shall be glad to return you the diamond before them!"

The comte felt his knees shake under him and a cold perspiration stood on his forehead.

He was ignorant of this peculiarity, and shivered, in spite of himself, at the thought of the danger which he had unconsciously incurred.

This man told the truth: he had the ring and, at any cost, it was necessary to snatch from him the proof of his crime.

"Well, sir," Zizi continued, growing impatient, "do you think that your ring isn't worth ten thousand francs?"

"But who told you all this?" murmured the comte, no longer trying to dissemble.

"A circular sent out in January by the Detective Bureau to all the jewelers at the request of the victim's heir."

Comte d'Abazoli-Viscosa made a gesture of rage. So, when he thought the affair of the Avenue d'Antin was definitely settled, here it was beginning again upon a new basis.

"Well," Zizi asked again, "have you decided? If not, I will offer the ring elsewhere . . . and all the information connected with it."

Then, lowering his voice, he added:

"Only I should be sorry to cause a colleague so much annoyance!"

"You have me by the throat," replied the other, yielding. "I am compelled to submit to your demands. You shall have your five hundred louis."

But he suddenly remembered that Nam was waiting in the darkness—Nam, whom, under the stress of his emotion, he had forgotten.

A smile flitted over his face. After all, what did the amount matter? Was not the Hindoo watching in the dusk with a knife? Recovering his composure, he said:

"You have brought the ring?"

"Come! come!" cried Zizi, slapping his companion's shoulder familiarly, "you don't think me simple enough for that? It is in a safe place. But, since we have reached an agreement, I will hold it at your disposal, at the hour and day you choose. Where shall we meet?"

"That is for you to arrange," replied the comte.

"Well, then, at your apartment, day after to-morrow morning, at ten o'clock. Does that suit you? You see, I have confidence. Besides, if by chance any misfortune happened to me, there are my associates, who would speak. Our exploit in the Rue Jadin would probably cost us a few months in prison, but the baron's murder would doubtless cost you more dearly. As to the secret of the engraved diamond," he added, "be sure

272

that it will be well kept; there is honor among thieves. Ah!" he sighed earnestly, "what interesting things we would have done if we had worked together!"

The comte was about to answer when, at that moment, the moon pierced the clouds, and a silvery ray fell upon the two men.

The comte, who had turned toward his companion, almost uttered a cry.

He knew the face—he remembered those features. Where had he seen this person? Or, rather, where had he encountered this profile of thoroughly feminine delicacy, this attractive, smiling face?

Suddenly a light darted through his brain. Yet he hesitated an instant, not believing the extraordinary revelation before his eyes. Still, such a resemblance was impossible to explain in any other way—he must bow before reality.

"Lady Dufferton!" he cried.

Now he understood everything. Lady Dufferton was a man. Lady Dufferton was the accomplice of the bold bandits of the Rue Jadin. Gliding into society under this disguise of a woman, she pointed out the deeds to be performed and helped them to accomplish them. It was she who at Krakowska's reception had opened the windows, unnoticed, at the right moment, after locking the doors, so that none of the guests could escape to give the alarm!

"You see, comrade," said Zizi gaily, "that we were made to understand each other! My petticoat is equal to your coronet, and the Indian army officer who serves as my absent husband is the worthy fellow-citizen of the Maharajah who has placed you in charge of his interests."

"Pardon me," the comte could not help protesting, striving to recover his footing in the midst of all he heard.

"Oh! no nonsense between us on this subject," replied the young man quickly; "no one knows how things go better than I . . . But you had a queer way of hiding in your safe to frighten burglars! Never mind! Only," he added, lowering his voice to a penitent tone, "if I had known that I was operating in a colleague's home, I wouldn't have taken so much useless trouble. Deuce, one should be forewarned. Come, my dear friend," he concluded, "let us shake hands with each other and, when we meet again, no longer work at cross purposes."

While Zizi was speaking, the comte was reflecting.

Henceforth, this man's life was sacred to him, and he must, at any cost, prevent Nam from executing his criminal designs.

274

Yet how was the Hindoo's arm to be stopped?
How was he to be warned that, through an unexpected change of affairs, they themselves were
the prisoners of the man whose disappearance
they desired.

So he said:

"Allow me to go with you a little distance . . ."

"Don't trouble yourself," replied Zizi, "I know
my way!"

"Yes," the comte persisted pleasantly. "I am
going to take a taxi, and I shall be glad to set
you down near your home."

Did Zizi still distrust his companion's intentions? Or had he, on the contrary, an intuition
that he had some special reason for not parting
from him in this way?

"The cars leave me just at my door," he answered.

But the comte did not yield the point.

"Very well, I'll take you to the nearest station."

They went out of the little dark avenue together.

Autos were passing in the Avenue: the comte
hailed one.

"To what station shall I take you?" he asked.

"To the Concorde: I shall take the North-
South."

Ten minutes later they reached it.

"Until day after to-morrow," said Zizi, shutting the door.

"I will expect you at ten o'clock." And the two men separated.

"Chauffeur," ordered the comte, "4 Rue Vézelay!" "Well," he added to himself, "I feel at ease now. He is safe. No doubt Nam understood that his intervention was useless. But, no matter, it is true to say that we never know what the future has in store. Matters which seem the most simple often prove the most complicated!"

CHAPTER XVIII

THE ANTAGONIST

FIFTEEN minutes later, Comte d'Abazoli-Viscosa was pacing restlessly up and down his office in the Rue Vézelay, waiting for Nam, when the latter appeared.

"Well," asked the Hindoo, who did not understand any detail of what had just happened, "what is it?"

In a few rapid words the comte informed him of his interview in the Champs-Elysées.

"Yes," he concluded, "we are at the mercy of unscrupulous individuals, whom nothing will prevent from selling the secret chance has placed in their hands to the man who, interested in knowing it, will buy it at whatever price they want!"

He took again several steps through the room, and went on bitterly:

"If you think we are not buried up to the neck this time, I really don't know what you would require! When Baron Plücke, once more bent on discovering the murderers of his uncle, has learned our part in the Avenue d'Antin affair, I am won-

'dering, even if we succeed in getting rid of the famous diamond, how we are to escape!"

He resumed his walk, nervously waving his arms, and continued:

"Ah! Nam, how true it is that when one has the imprudence to put the little finger into machinery, it isn't long before the whole body is drawn in. Who would have supposed, when I began to steal the money of my employer's customers, that I should so soon have become a murderer? From crime to crime, where shall we end? Or, rather, where will you drag me? Answer me, Nam," he exclaimed angrily, enraged by the obstinate silence of his companion, "answer me!"

But the Hindoo, seated in an armchair, listened impassively, looking at him with his little sparkling eyes, not a line of his face betraying the slightest emotion.

"If you were satisfied," he murmured at last, "with earning all your life a hundred francs a month in an out-of-the-way corner of the provinces, why didn't you stay there?"

The comte found no answer. Nam was right: this was no time for scruples or remorse; he ought to have measured in former days the depth of the gulf over which he was leaning. Now it was too late to draw back, nothing could stop his descent of the slope on which he had so imprudently ventured.

The two accomplices remained for an instant face to face, looking at each other.

The gentleman, with contracted brows, haggard face, pale, with an expression of anguish in his eyes, seemed like a hopeless man, who feels destruction hovering above his head; the Hindoo, on the contrary, cool, calm, appeared like a wrestler confident of victory, and sure of himself.

"And now," asked the comte, "what do you expect to do?"

"It is very simple," replied Nam quietly. "In the first place, I shall not excite myself uselessly. Then I shall carefully examine the situation. Let us reason an instant. From what quarter is the danger coming? Those persons of whom you are in such fear? No. They will no more denounce the murderers of the Avenue d'Antin, than we shall the wall-cutters of the Rue Vézelay. To inform against us, as you have said, they would need to be pressed by an irresistible necessity for money. The ten thousand francs which we are going to give them in exchange for the ring will close their lips for some time, and, meanwhile, I hope to have found a way to extricate ourselves from the affair. There is only one man from whom we have everything to fear. That man is Baron

Plücke. He alone is interested in delivering us to justice. Very well," he added, emphatically, "Baron Plücke shall disappear and, like Lucien Delorme, he will carry into a better world a secret that brings misfortune to all who possess it."

"Nam," murmured the comte, shaking his head, "how cheaply you hold human life!"

"Pshaw, were we not, in this very spot . . ."

"So many things have happened since! Now, Baron Plücke has no reason to come to this house. Without mentioning, besides, that while the investigation of the robbery of the jewels was going on, our safe being sealed, has not yet been repaired, and a dead body would be terribly in our way."

"So," Nam said calmly, "the baron's will not leave his office."

"A dangerous adventure! No doubt it will be easy for you to reach him. He receives everyone, according to the custom of American business men, but getting in is not all. The baron is well guarded, and it is certain that with strangers he will take every precaution."

"Don't worry," replied the Hindoo, "I will not risk myself there."

The comte turned pale.

"Are you depending upon me?"

The other shrugged his shoulders.

"No," he answered, laughing; "I know you cannot bear the sight of blood and that your hand would shake."

He reflected an instant, and then continued:

"I have a better plan. Baron Plücke will disappear without the need of our exposing ourselves uselessly."

"Do you intend to draw him into some ambush? You saw this evening that this method is not infallible. And once the baron's suspicion is aroused . . ."

"Don't question me any farther," replied the Hindoo. "You shall know everything to-morrow. Meanwhile sleep peacefully. You are one of the people who require sleep to regain their composure and coolness!"

Without adding anything more, Nam withdrew.

It was afternoon on the following day when he returned. The comte had just risen, after a sleepless night, during which he had not closed his eyes until the first rays of the sun had flecked his shutters with gold, and was waiting for him with feverish impatience.

"Well," he asked, as he saw him, "what have you done?"

The other's answer was to place on a night-table the little wooden box he held in his hands:

"This is the thing," he said.

"What is it?" asked the comte, coming forward curiously.

"My last night's work; I haven't wasted my time, have I, while you were sleeping? Wouldn't anyone suppose that it was one of those boxes in which, at the holiday season, confectioners send their gifts?"

"I understand," cried the comte; "you are going to send Baron Plücke some poisoned bonbons which——"

"No," replied the Hindoo, "that is an expedient for a melodrama that even a child would suspect. There is nothing remarkable about this box, except that when an attempt to open it is made something unexpected happens. It explodes and reduces to fragments the imprudent person who wanted to see what it contained."

"So you know how to make bombs, Nam?" cried the comte.

Nam's face assumed a modest expression:

"When one lives on the edge of society, one must know a little of everything."

"And, with this, you will doubtless blow up the house in which the baron is living?"

"Why the house? Isn't he himself enough for us?"

"Granted; but how will you manage it?"

The Hindoo began to laugh, that sinister laugh with which he emphasized all his crimes.

"In the simplest way in the world—by making the baron open my box himself."

"A difficult matter!" exclaimed the other, shaking his head incredulously.

"No, with a little imagination we reach everything. Do you want to know how I shall proceed? Very well, then, listen."

Nam took his time and, looking his colleague steadily in the eyes, as if to read his impressions, went on slowly:

"Presently, someone will go up the baron's stairs, after having ascertained positively that the latter is out. He will carry this box and a letter and, apparently, much vexed by the master's absence, will tell the servant who opens the door to be sure to place both in the right hands."

"Well," interrupted the comte, "but . . ."

"Wait a little while. When the baron returns he will of course receive the two articles at once, with the message. Puzzled, he will unseal the letter and what will he see?"

The Hindoo drew from his pocket an envelope and, taking from it a sheet of paper, handed it to the comte, who read the contents aloud.

"M. Le Baron,
    "The signers of this letter are the men who broke open Comte d'Abazoli-Viscosa's safe, and took possession of the jewels it contained."

"Think how startled he'll be!" put in Nam.

    "To-day [the comte went on] less through remorse than from the difficulty which they experience in getting rid of them without risk to themselves, as you will understand, they have determined to address you, not being ignorant of your dealings with Comte d'Abazoli-Viscosa to buy them from him . . ."

Here he interrupted himself with the objection: "They are well informed!"

"And why not?" replied Nam calmly. "Were they not still better informed to have stolen the gems the very evening before the day that they were to be delivered?"

"That is true." And he continued:

    "They know that you are too good a business man to be ignorant that all trouble must be paid for. So they leave to your generosity the matter of naming the amount of the sum which you will deduct from your profits in this transaction, to reward their act. They will be satisfied with the check you send to X. Y. Z. 234, Bureau No. 65, and the promise on honor that you will not inform the police and which you will publish, under the same initials, in the *Press* of next Friday.

"Thanking you in advance, M. le Baron, for your kindness to them,

"Very respectfully yours,

"THE BROTHERS OF MONTPARNO."

"Well?" asked Nam.

"Upon my word, it is cleverly imagined: but it would be necessary to have the baron open the box himself."

"Don't worry on that score. Curiosity will conquer prudence. And even if a servant or a secretary forces the lid open with a chisel, the baron will be, nevertheless, at his side, leaning intently over the box. When the point in question is the Maharajah's jewels, worth fifty millions . . ."

The comte remained silent a moment, reflecting.

"And," he asked, "will he not wonder why the robbers addressed themselves to him, instead of to Comte d'Abazoli-Viscosa?"

"Baron Plücke is far too shrewd not to perceive that, having the jewels in his hands, he will be able to obtain far better terms from the man with whom he is treating, and not to be aware that his correspondents expect that he will know how to recognize the advantage which they thus afford him."

"That's so."

"Now," said Nam, "let us act without delay. To-morrow, when our fine fellow comes with the ring, we must be able to inform him that we have nothing more to fear from the baron, and any blackmail from that quarter will be useless!"

"Let us act then," replied the comte, now convinced. "What am I to do?"

"This. While I am making up, put on my goat-skin coat, and my cap and goggles. In this disguise you will go with the auto to stand in front of the baron's house. He is a man of regular habits, didn't you tell me? Every day, after luncheon, he goes to his business on foot?"

"Yes."

"Then you will watch to see if he goes out."

"And if he does?"

"You will get down from your seat and stand beside your car, like a patient servant waiting for his master. I shall see you as I pass, and know that I can go up."

"And in the contrary case?"

"You won't stir from your wheel. I'll keep near, ready to come as soon as you have signaled that the coast is clear."

While speaking he had taken from his apron a sheet of paper and a piece of cord.

"Now you must help me."

"To do what?"

"To wrap this box. It must be presented in an attractive way. Don't you know the proverb that the manner of giving is worth more than the gift?"

But the comte had been unable to repress an involuntary shrinking.

"Coward!" exclaimed Nam. "The explosion cannot take place unless the lid is raised!"

"You are sure of that?"

"I'll answer for it," replied the Hindoo peremptorily: "I have no more desire to be blown up than you have."

Five minutes after, while Comte d'Abazoli-Viscosa, dressed as a chauffeur, was getting into his auto, which Nam had brought to the door before he woke, the Hindoo, standing before the glass in the dressing-room, was occupied in altering his appearance.

An excellent paint had soon changed the tawny hue of his complexion into the ruddy tint of a Parisian workman who was fond of loitering at the cafés in his quarter; a little fair goatee flourished under his chin; a wig of the same color completed the transformation and, lastly, he put on a neat simple suit which gave him the appearance of a respectable messenger.

Then, with his box under his arm, he quietly reached the street by the servants' staircase, without being noticed by the janitor as he passed out, and walked slowly toward the Champs-Elysées.

The auto was in front of the financier's house, and the comte was standing beside it. So the baron had gone out.

Chance favored the Hindoo.

He soon came down with empty hands and walked quietly away, while his employer, starting his motor, returned to the Rue Vézelay.

Fifteen minutes later, the two accomplices found themselves face to face.

"The thing is done," said Nam, removing his make-up. "The baron, I was told, would return at five o'clock. The man promised to give him the letter and the box at once. Go to your club, as you do every day, without changing any of your habits; I will stroll around the house to be the first to hear the explosion. You can imagine the stir it will make throughout the quarter!"

CHAPTER XIX

EXPLANATION OF THE MOST EXTRAORDINARY PHENOMENON

FIVE o'clock had just struck when Baron Plücke, who had an appointment with his architect, returned home.

"During your absence, M. le Baron," said his valet, who had hastened to open the door for him, "a messenger brought this package and letter, which he urged me to deliver to you at once."

The financier carelessly opened the letter, at which he cast a rapid glance.

Instantly, as Nam had predicted, his face expressed the greatest surprise, and he reread, line by line, for the second time, the singular missive.

"It is not possible!" he murmured.

And, without taking time to give the servant his overcoat and hat, he hurried to his office with the precious box, asking:

"Is my secretary here?"

"Yes, M. le Baron."

"Ask him to come to me at once."

But the valet said:

"There is also a young man who has been waiting an hour. As he insisted upon seeing you without delay, saying that you knew him, I showed
him into the drawing-room."

The financier was about to give him an order
to dismiss the intruder, when his eye fell on the
name engraved on the card his servant was offering on a silver waiter.

"Lucien Delorme!" he exclaimed, more and
more amazed.

And, recalling the conversation he had had concerning him a few days before with the head of
the detective service, he added:

"What can he want of me? Very well," he
added aloud, "I will see him as I pass."

Carrying under his arm the precious box, he
went toward the room into which his visitor had
been shown.

Lucien Delorme had rushed like a madman from
the Hôtel des Nouvelles-Hébrides, after placing
in his bed the body of poor M. Boistet, and ar-
ranging a scene intended to deceive the persons
who were evidently determined not to lose an instant in ridding themselves of him at any cost.

The next morning the story of his assassina-
tion in the newspapers had showed him that his
precautions had not been futile.

For a week he had remained hidden at the

other end of Paris, not daring to go out, and wondering what he was to do henceforth to escape the pursuit of the criminals.

Undoubtedly, for the time, they believed him dead. But this could not last. Even with the best fortune, was he not at the mercy of an accidental meeting or a malevolent chance?

Go back to his mother?

But was it not in leaving Eu that he had met this woman who, in league with them, had tried to win his secret from him and led him into an ambush? This suggested that they had some branch in that city and that his return would be immediately announced to them.

Inform the police?

He remembered the welcome he had received from M. Clamart when he had tried to unmask Comte d'Abazoli-Viscosa, and did not care to brave, a second time, his sarcastic comments.

Only one man could aid him, the man who had an interest in discovering his uncle's murderers, in knowing the prodigious swindle to which he had almost fallen a victim.

He did not hesitate, and decided to go without delay to Baron Plücke to ask his assistance.

When he arrived at the Avenue des Champs-Elysées that day, the two accomplices had just gone away and did not see him enter the financier's home.

Meanwhile, the baron had entered the drawing-room and, curious to know the reason for such a visit, after all that M. Clamart had told him, he asked:

"You wish to speak to me, sir?"

"M. le Baron," replied the young man, "I will tell you later the causes of a disappearance which must have surprised you. Now, I am simply bringing you the result of the investigation which you desired me to undertake."

In spite of his self-control, the baron could not help a gesture of intense astonishment.

"I am listening, sir," he said.

"The murderer of your uncle," Lucien Delorme continued, "is no other than the individual who offered to sell you jewels which exist solely in his imagination."

"Sir," replied the other in a cold tone, tinged with a shade of sarcasm, "it would be an unworthy act if I were to ring for my servants and turn you over to the police, who are seeking for you. Yet, nevertheless, I wish to warn you that it is useless to try to dupe me or to believe me ignorant of your identity, and your purpose in coming here. A single remark will destroy all your falsehoods in advance: these

292

jewels, which you use to make a false accusation against an honest man, actually exist, and the proof . . ."

He rapped on the box under his arm and added:

" . . . is that they are here!"

But Lucien Delorme, who had pushed his glasses up on his forehead and looked keenly at the box a moment, answered quietly:

"Put it on the table, sir, and do not touch it again. It does not contain precious stones; but watch-springs, cylinders, and explosives. In short, it is a bomb which will burst at the first shock!"

"Oh!" cried the baron, astounded by what he heard, "what do you know about it?"

"I see it . . . as I see," he continued, "that the left pocket of your vest contains a large flat watch, the one opposite a little metal portmonnaie for gold; in your side pocket is a folded eyeglass, under your glove, on your ring-finger, a ring in the shape of a serpent, and even, in your jaw, two incisors and three canines filled with gold—is this correct?"

"So you see everything?" exclaimed the bewildered baron.

"Yes, M. le Baron, I see through bodies and through things . . . I see through walls!"

"But how?"

"Will you take the trouble to listen to me a moment?"

Then as his host, by a gesture, had motioned him to an armchair, he sat down and began this singular story.

"Several months ago, one morning, I started for Dieppe. By my mother's advice, I was going to consult Dr. Trémeaux. A little red spot, caused I don't know how, disfigured my right nostril. My aunt, who lives in Dieppe with my cousin Marise, had spoken of a surgeon who worked wonders with radio-electric machines of his own invention to cure this kind of little physical ailment.

"I left his office delighted with the success of the operation, and was returning to my aunt's, where I was to lunch, not without drawing from my pocket, every now and then, a little mirror and looking at myself a moment with satisfaction.

"This thought was doubtless occupying my mind more than I admitted for, suddenly, in crossing a street, I did not see the sidewalk, missed my footing, and fell full length while my eyeglasses slid from my nose, and my cane and hat rolled on the ground.

"Luckily, the fall did me no injury. I was
294

soon on my feet again. But the accident had the most unexpected consequences.

"I looked around me with wild eyes. Great drops of perspiration stood on my forehead. My face expressed terrible agony. My whole body shuddered with horror and broken words fell from my lips.

"Skeletons! . . . skeletons everywhere! . . . walking on the sidewalk . . . driving the carriages . . . on all the stories of the houses. . .

"My cries of alarm had caused a natural stir in the street.

"People ran toward me, while my exclamations increased:

" 'Now they are coming toward me . . . here they are! . . . their bony arms are stretched toward me . . . Oh, don't come near me, skeletons . . . don't touch me!'

"I wanted to fly, but my limbs refused to carry me.

"Then I fell on the edge of the sidewalk, dazed, panting, covering my eyes with my trembling hands, as if to shut out a horrible vision.

"Yet this moment's prostration had calmed me. With the mechanical gesture of a near-sighted person, I had put on my glasses again and, raising my head, I looked with surprise at the crowd surrounding me.

" 'Oh!' I muttered under my breath, 'what caused this?—what is the meaning of the hallucination I had so suddenly?'

" 'Take a carriage, and return home,' one of the spectators advised me in a fatherly way, as he helped me to rise. 'These attacks of vertigo are frequent after overwork; you need rest.'

"Just then, a cab came up; I jumped in, calling my aunt's address to the driver.

"While he was lashing his horses I wiped the perspiration from my forehead with my handkerchief, brushed the dust from my hat, and then tried to reduce my thoughts to order.

" 'The clearest thing in the matter,' I thought, 'is that I have been punished for not paying attention. When my aunt hears this she will make fun of me again, treating me as if I were absent-minded. In fact,' I instantly added, 'in order not to alarm her uselessly, I won't tell her anything about this strange adventure!'

"When I reached her house I was most cordially received, as usual; my cousin offered me cheeks to kiss as fresh as two ripe peaches.

"But, just as I was going to embrace her, the cord of my eyeglasses caught in my cuff-button and dragged them from my nose; at the same time I uttered a cry of terror, stammering, and bewildered.

" 'Oh, Good Lord, Marise, too, changed into a skeleton . . . and my aunt . . . and the little dog . . . the little dog also . . . Begone, phantoms—you specters that pursue me everywhere!'

"Fairly maddened, I fled, ran across the antechamber, dashed downstairs four steps at a time, and reached the janitress's room like an avalanche.

"The good woman was knitting quietly behind her glass door.

"I darted toward her:

" 'Help!'

"But I had not crossed the threshold when I started back with a gesture of horror:

"Another one!

"And this time I fell fainting on the floor."

Lucien Delorme stopped a moment to take breath: then, while Baron Plücke looked at him anxiously, thinking himself in the presence of a madman, he continued:

"Night had come when, a few hours later, I recovered my senses.

"I was lying with my head covered with thick bandages. I felt sore all over. My forehead ached confusedly. My ideas were muddled, and I vainly sought to regain a little clearness of mind.

"At my first movement a little soft hand was

laid on my burning fingers, while my cousin's voice murmured:

" 'Don't stir, Lucien. Don't speak, that is forbidden. We are taking care of you in our house. Your mother arrived just now. We telegraphed to her. Oh, my poor cousin, what a fright you gave us when you were picked up in the janitress's room, with your face covered with blood. Dr. Trémeaux, who came at once, feared concussion of the brain.'

" 'Here he comes now,' interrupted my aunt.

"The door was closing upon the physician who, approaching my bed, leaned over me.

" 'Let us see how we are this evening. No agitation! Good . . . Give me your wrist. Excellent,' he added, at the end of an instant; 'there is no fever. I will remove the ban of silence. Now, let us talk a little, for these ladies have told me such tragical things . . .'

" 'Alas, Doctor,' I cried, 'they have told only the truth!'

"While I was relating all that had happened since my fall, Dr. Trémeaux shook his head, looking at Marise and my aunt; it was evident that he was wondering whether the delirium was not continuing, and if it was not my mental condition that most required his care.

" 'Come,' he answered in a fatherly tone, 'I am

going to examine the little cuts on your skull. We'll attend to this skeleton story later.'

"While speaking, he was unfastening the bandages, then he lifted the piece of gutta percha, but at the very moment that he removed the bandages, wet with cold water, the electricity went out, and the room was plunged in darkness.

" 'Those fuses have burst again!' exclaimed my aunt.

"But while she rushed out to get a lamp, my cousin and the doctor stood motionless with bewilderment, asking themselves if they, too, were not the victims, in their turn, of a hallucination: before them, on my bed, two phosphorescent spots pierced the darkness.

"The physician, recovering his coolness, was trying to discover with his fingers the exact place from which these twin lights could proceed, when he suddenly uttered a stifled exclamation:

" 'Why, it is his eyes that are luminous! One would say that they produced a sort of X-ray.'

" 'X-ray?' repeated Marise bewildered.

" 'It is not possible,' continued the practician, under his breath, as if he were talking to himself. 'One would have to suppose the improbable hypothesis that he has swallowed a tube of radium! . . .'

" 'Doctor,' I interrupted, laughing, 'at the price

per gramme, my means would not allow me to indulge in such banquets!'

" 'Who is talking of them?' retorted the physician. 'Has the human body the capacity to absorb only through deglutition? But,' he added instantly, 'often a pleasant philosophy is right in affirming that truth always progresses through error; here is an objection that perhaps will put us on the right track! Wasn't it this morning that you came to my office for me to remove a small sanguino-vascular growth from your nostril?'

" 'This very morning, Doctor.'

" 'I applied a dressing?'

" 'Yes.'

" 'Which, according to my treatment, was an application of radium. Well, then,' he continued, growing animated, 'we may suppose that an infinitesimal atom was detached, penetrated under your skin, lodged in a corner of your nose . . .'

" 'But, Doctor, that isn't the way we see!'

" 'Wait. This atom of radium was drawn in, carried along by the circulatory stream. The violent shock of your fall localized it in your brain, at the end of some vessel without an outlet. Your skull has become a radiographic apparatus. You see with X-rays!'

300

" 'But the skeletons !' I cried, astounded by what I heard . . . 'the skeletons?'

" 'Are you ignorant of the first elements of radioscopy?' asked the physician. 'As they are capable of penetrating stones, wood, paper, walls, your gaze can see nothing in human beings except their bones. Oh, my friend,' he added, enthusiastically, 'you are a unique phenomenon, the first man to whom so marvelous a faculty has been given !'

" 'Am I then condemned to live in a cemetery, Doctor,' I asked, 'and is there no way of saving me from this perpetual spectacle of horror?"

" 'It will suffice to place before your eyes a body refractory to the X-rays, such as silver, mercury, or glass . . .'

"The last word made me start. Now everything was explained, and I understood all."

"It was my eyeglasses, it was the window of the cab, it was the panes of the janitress's door which had restored their human form to the pedestrians, to the inhabitants of the houses, to Marise, to the janitress; but as soon as I no longer looked at them through this simple, fragile protector, they again became to me horrible skeletons. And if, on my awakening, I had not seen my cousin, my aunt, and the doctor under this form, through the bands of linen which enveloped my head, it was because the water wetting the compresses on my face contained salts of lead, which the X-rays cannot pass!"

Baron Plücke gazed at the speaker with an amazement which he no longer attempted to conceal.

Extraordinary as the whole story to which he had just listened might be, yet he could not do otherwise than believe it.

Once more truth was not probable.

Then, as he entreated him to do so, Lucien Delorme told him the whole story of all his agitated life, from the day when, arriving in Paris to consult a prince of science concerning his extraordinary case, he had gone to Madame Armelin's family boarding-house.

He explained how, lying awake all night, thinking sadly of the singularity of his fate, he had seen, behind the wall, as if on a radioscopic screen, two skeletons enter the room next to his own, the taller having a bullet in his skull, the shorter man one in his leg, and strangle the old American lady with a cord which must certainly be of steel, since the X-rays had not passed through it. So, in spite of M. Clamart's incredulity, he had witnessed all the details of the murder with such precision that he had believed himself to be

302

having a nightmare, and it was only the following morning, on hearing of the crime which had been committed, that he had understood he had not been dreaming.

He also told him how, after having tried, at his request, to find the murderers of the Avenue d'Antin, he had met, by accident, on the day that he came to his house to inform him that he would give up the commission, Comte d'Abazoli-Viscosa, and perceived, with amazement, that the latter carried in the same part of the skull as Mrs. Tankery's murderer the indelible mark which would have led to his recognition among a hundred thousand, how before allowing his employer to enter a business transaction with a scoundrel of this kind, he had determined to find out whether the Maharajah's jewels really existed, delaying the appointment between the two men by a simple telephone message from one to the other, how, after having discovered that the safe was empty, he had been shut up in it, seeing the comte and his servant close the iron blinds, turn the keys of the doors, carry away his coat, which he easily recognized by the buttons, one of which, on the right side, was missing, and how, finally, that very evening, at the time when he no longer expected anything but a horrible death, some shrewd wall-cutters had rescued him and fled before the sudden appearance, in the darkness, of his luminous eyes.

Lucien told him how, at the restaurant of the Silver Pike, having taken off his glasses to remove the mist on them, he had seen, distinctly, in the same way, the skeleton of his fiancée pour the contents of a metal vial into his glass and, descending hurriedly, overwhelmed by this sudden revelation he had recognized the Hindoo under his disguise of an old woman selling flowers, by the bullet in the leg which marked him also with an indelible sign.

"Comte d'Abazoli-Viscosa," he concluded, "and his accomplice, Nam, are nothing but two abominable rascals, whom I have come to ask you, sir, to help me unmask."

"I promise it," cried the baron. "But," he added instantly, panting for breath, almost crushed by these revelations, "you are a unique phenomenon and your fortune is made!"

Lucien Delorme shook his head mournfully:

"No," he replied, "for I have not told you all. I have told you that I came to Paris to consult a master of science, but you do not know his verdict. The veil of Isis cannot be raised with impunity, M. le Baron, and Nature always takes her revenge upon the man who has penetrated her mystery! The radium in my brain is slowly destroying the different layers in contact with it. There will be first convulsions, then the progressive disappearance of reason and, finally, death through exhaustion."

"But," exclaimed the financier, "is there no remedy? Cannot you have this dangerous substance removed by an operation?"

"An operation would cause instantaneously what will happen only gradually, for the surgeon's scalpel would have to remove, slice by slice, the portions of cerebral matter containing the particle of radium."

He paused an instant and, sighing mournfully, continued:

"Yet, for a moment, love had blinded me to the degree of making me forget my terrible fate; the kisses of a worshiped fiancée had, in spite of myself, restored hope. I will not tell you the disillusion which awaited me, nor the cruel suffering that now makes death appear as a deliverance."

The baron had risen and, holding out his hand to the young man, said:

"However that may be, my friend, you have done me a great service and I will keep the promise I made you. To-morrow the check for two hundred thousand francs which were to be paid for the clews that would have permitted me to discover my uncle's assassins will be at your disposal."

"I will accept it," replied Lucien simply, "not for myself, but for my mother. This sum will bring a little cheer into her life, crushed by my disappearance from the world."

"But why should you not go to her?" asked the baron.

"Because my duty forbids it. I am going to become a public peril. Gradually I shall become, in my turn, radio-active, and all who approach me will undergo the effects of this formidable body. To live with me would be to rush to a slow death."

Then, with an energetic gesture, stopping the exclamation on the baron's lips, he added:

"Now, time presses, let us hasten to the police office; let us rid society of these two scoundrels!"

CHAPTER XX

IMMANENT JUSTICE

WHEN, accompanied by the financier to the head of the detective service, Lucien Delorme had finished, for the second time, his long story, M. Clamart was compelled to yield to the evidence, admit the reality of the criminal maneuvers of which the young man had been the victim at the hands of Comte d'Abazoli-Viscosa and his servant, and recognize them as two miserable murderers.

One point, however, still remained obscure to him.

"Now, then, sir," he asked, "how did you come into connection with the comte's maid?"

"What maid?"

M. Clamart showed him the brooch containing Juliette's photograph, which had been found in searching the Hôtel des Nouvelles Hébrides.

"Why, that is Georgette!" exclaimed Lucien Delorme, glancing at it. "What! She was in the comte's service? Then that explains everything!"

And he told the police officer all the particulars of his love affair with the young girl whom he had met in the train from Eu.

"Everything is explained," replied M. Clamart, shaking his head incredulously, "except why, on the very day I went to the Rue Vézelay, that woman was murdered in her employer's kitchen."

Lucien Delorme rose, deadly pale.

"Georgette murdered!" he faltered . . . "and by whom?"

"That is what we are vainly trying to discover, sir! There is an impenetrable mystery hovering over this strange affair which we shall end by piercing! But, however that may be," he added, turning to the baron, "the exploits of these two knaves have lasted long enough! To-morrow morning we will arrest them, and we shall take every precaution that they do not escape!"

Lucien Delorme was overwhelmed by the news of Georgette's death. In the depths of his soul did he still love his former fiancée? Did he still hope, in spite of everything, for one of those miracles usual in love? . . . fathomless mystery of the human heart! . . . and now that all was over, that he was never to see the young girl more, it seemed as if everything was crumbling around him, and the last bond that attached him to life was breaking.

"M. Clamart," he said, "I have a favor to ask —will you allow me to go to the comte's house before your men, and speak to him a moment, alone, face to face? I have vengeance to take on this miscreant for something, and if you will let me I will take him back his bomb!"

"Very well," replied the other, to whom the pluck of this action appealed—go to the Rue Vézelay to-morrow morning at ten o'clock."

"I'll be there."

While M. Clamart was accompanying his callers, Nam had returned to the Avenue des Champs-Elysées, directly after the departure of his employer for the club.

Posted not far off, behind a tree, he had seen, by the flickering light of a gas jet, the financier's auto stop before the house and the latter get out of it to enter, without discovering that in the back of the car sat Lucien Delorme, whom the chauffeur had orders to take to the hotel where he had sought refuge, at the other end of Paris.

"The explosion will take place in a few minutes," muttered the Hindoo.

But minutes had passed—then hours—a part of the night—and the bomb had not yet burst.

"What can be the trouble?" Nam asked himself anxiously, far from suspecting the truth. "Has not the detonator acted—has the baron mistrusted anything—or has he merely deferred opening the precious casket until another day?"

All these conjectures were plausible and, the next day, in his employer's office, the Hindoo, not knowing what to think, was discussing them with him.

"Yet," he repeated obstinately, "it is impossible that the bomb should have proved a failure! —impossible! Suppose that, under some pretext, you should go up to the baron's office to see what is happening?"

"So that he may offer to open the box in my presence," replied the comte. "Thank you kindly!"

The arrival of Zizi interrupted the conversation.

"Good-morning, my dear comte, he said cordially, "you see I am prompt in coming to you!"

Looking around him, he added, smiling:

"There has been no change since the day when you were kind enough to have tea served to Lady Dufferton and some of her friends, to whom you showed the famous safe."

"You have the ring?" said the comte, without appearing to have heard his words.

"Yes."

Holding out his hand, Zizi showed it to him on his middle finger.

"My fingers are smaller than yours!" he explained.

The comte opened a drawer in his desk, took from it a roll of bank bills, pinned together, counted them rapidly and, putting them on the table, said:

"Here are the ten thousand francs. But wait an instant, if you please!" he added, as Zizi was already advancing to take them. "We have one last point to discuss. Large as was the sum you asked for my jewel, I paid it without discussion."

Then, as Zizi, with a little knowing air, nodded assent, he went on:

"Let me tell you, sir, that I have other reasons for that than those you suppose. Only we are talking here like people who know the value of words, and it is thoroughly understood, isn't it, that we are dealing honestly? With this diamond I am buying your absolute silence?"

"Sir," replied Zizi quickly, as if such a question had been an insult, "I am not one of those people who betray a secret that does not belong to them."

He was drawing the ring from his finger to deliver it to the comte, when the bell rang:

"Nam," exclaimed the latter, "get rid of this intruder!"

But an instant after the Hindoo reappeared,

his features convulsed, his face expressing intense amazement.

"It's he," he stammered . . . "he, the man with the glasses, still alive!"

"Lucien Delorme?" cried the comte, dazed in his turn.

But Nam, who had gone to the window, went on:

"And the police behind him!"

"The police!" repeated Zizi, who did not understand what was happening.

"I'm not mistaken . . . look at those men slouching along the street, casting furtive glances toward our house. I know them well, they are detectives, they are only waiting for a signal to enter!"

"Every man for himself!" cried the comte.

"No," replied Nam vehemently—"to fly is to confess guilt—Comte d'Abazoli-Viscosa must brave the storm. Lost or not, we must fight to the end. Can one ever know the result of a battle? But the important thing," he concluded, turning to Zizi, "is that you should vanish with the engraved diamond—we will meet again later."

"Willingly," replied the other, who had no inclination to meet police officers. "But how? Your house is undoubtedly surrounded! To jump out of the window would mean surely falling into their hands. Hiding me in some closet would be equally useless, for you know that they will search everywhere."

"Wait!" cried Nam.

Taking a bunch of keys on the comte's desk, he opened the safe.

"Go in there—the back has not been replaced—from the other side you will find yourself in the next house—you will not be looked for there, and it will be easy to go out quietly when all danger is over."

"I know those places!" exclaimed Zizi, hastening to obey. "At any rate," he added, "you may be sure that, happen what may, I will not betray you!"

"Hang it," muttered the Hindoo, shutting the steel door upon him, "what a pity that the safe wasn't repaired: we should be rid forever of this disturber! Now I'll bring in Lucien Delorme, and we shall see what he wants from us."

The young man entered with a calm, resolute air, carrying under his arm the casket which he placed on a chair near the door.

Then, advancing two steps toward the comte, he folded his arms, and said slowly:

"Now I will settle with you . . . !"

But he did not finish.

Nam had glided behind him to the box and introducing with a swift, steady movement, the blade of a knife under the lid, he pressed upon it with all his strength.

Instantly there was a terrible explosion which shook the whole street, and shattered all the panes of glass in the neighboring houses.

When, a few seconds later, the police, following M. Clamart, entered the office, they found only a shapeless mass of bones and flesh.

It was all that remained of Comte d'Abazoli-Viscosa, Nam, and Lucien Delorme, the first man to whom had been given the superhuman faculty of *seeing through walls* . . .

Arcachon, 1912.

(3)

THE END

www.ingramcontent.com/pod-product-compliance
Lightning Source LLC
Chambersburg PA
CBHW032205030726
47494CB00020B/619